"...ly we're watching," a rough voice said when I answered the phone. "You're not safe, you know. We can go wherever you go. No matter where you are, or what you do, we'll get you if you don't leave it alone. Now, leave it be or you'll be dead."

I gasped. "Leave what be?"

"Don't act stupid. We know you're not. You're too smart for your own good. And if you call the police again, or tell anyone about this, you're gonna be history."

The line went dead and I dropped the receiver into the cradle as if it were too hot to handle. I was sweating, chilled and scared. Too hot to handle? That was an apt phrase. I felt like writing it down to remind me of the rough-tough voice on the phone and his message. I was sure I should quit while I was behind and still alive.

Available from Crosswinds

Bigger is Better
by Sheila Schwartz

Sylvia Smith-Smith
by Peter Nelson

The Gifting
by Ann Gabhart

THE EYE OF THE STORM

SUSAN DODSON

═══CROSSWINDS

New York • Toronto
Sydney • Auckland
Manila

With much love for my parents,
Charles and Louise,
and for Betsy, Judy and Bill
whom they also produced.

First publication October 1987

ISBN 0-373-98010-8

Copyright © 1987 by Susan Dodson

All rights reserved. Australian copyright 1987. New Zealand copyright 1987. Philippine copyright 1987. Except for use in any review, the reproduction or utilization of this work in whole or in part in any form by any electronic, mechanical or other means, now known or hereafter invented, including xerography, photocopying and recording, or in any information storage or retrieval system, is forbidden without the permission of the publisher, Crosswinds, 300 East 42nd St., New York, N.Y. 10017

All the characters in this book are fictitious. Any resemblance to actual persons, living or dead, is purely coincidental.

Crosswinds is a registered trademark of the publisher.

Printed in the U.S.A.

RL 5.8, IL age 12 and up

SUSAN DODSON

After having worked as an artist for a number of years, Susan Dodson began her writing career in a class at Hunter College. She says the greatest influence on her writing has been reading. "Mysteries have always been my great love," adds Dodson, who is a member of the board of directors of Mystery Writers of America. She is the author of five acclaimed books for young adults, including *The Creep, Have You Seen This Girl?* and *Shadows Across the Sand.*

Chapter One

I hurried to Community General Hospital as soon as I saw the hurricane warnings on television. My mother tried to stop me, pointing out, "Tessa! You haven't been there long enough to do any good! There are other TeeVees who have lots more experience."

"True," I answered, going out the door. "But I can still help and I want to."

Short of running after the car and hanging on to the front bumper, there wasn't much she could do but let me go. I have my own car. Well, really, it's my brother Tim's. But he's spending a year at the Sorbonne in Paris. Lucky him, but lucky me too, to have on loan his Volkswagen bug, fifteen years old, painted a screaming blue, and lovingly rebuilt.

I shifted gears, backed out of the driveway, and tooted the weird trumpet horn at Mom, who was busy taping the living-room windows. Last year it had taken us days to get the gunk off, but she would doggedly do it again.

The wind was already blowing wildly as I turned on the car radio to get the news. This hurricane was the first of the season, the newscaster said, as though everyone in Lake Watson, Texas, didn't already know that. But Tropical Storm Aaron had been reclassified as a hurricane, and although he was supposed to hit Louisiana, instead of southern Texas, he changed his course. I think they used to call hurricanes by female names because they are fickle and flighty; maybe we have come a long way.

I got into a bottleneck on the highway near the exit to Houston, seventy miles to the north. Yep, the evacuees were on their way. I was sure that would leave the hospital shorthanded, and I was antsy to get going.

But I was stuck, locked into place for fifteen minutes. The wind was making the trees dance, and the sky was darkening. I turned on the headlights, trying to pretend I wasn't scared, but hurricanes were new to me. The only one I'd been through before, I'd spent safe at home. My new home, that is. I'd only lived in Texas since the previous August, and now it was the third week of June. Almost a year, but what a year.

First my dad, a well-known physician, had suddenly decided to sell his practice in Michigan and move us to Texas. He's an internist, although he's always harbored the idea of being a family practitioner. In Lake Watson, there was a brand-new hospital and few doctors. He saw it as a chance at another beginning; my mother, at first, referred to it as a mid-life crisis.

My new school had been so hard to adjust to that for a small time, I wasn't very nice to live with. But when winter came, if it can be called that, and I didn't need coats, boots, leg warmers or gloves, I changed my mind. There were a few cold spells, but nothing like Michigan, and I loved being warm too much to be nasty about the move for long. Of course the lake in Lake Watson is more like a pond compared to Lake Michigan, but on the other hand, who needs frigid air blowing down their necks for four months?

Talk about blows, though, it was a low one when my big bro, Tim, got a grant to study in Paris. Tim is an artist, like my mother, and yet he has a practical side. One day, he plans to become a great painter. In the meantime he's studying art restoration, which will mean a salary, eventually.

I'd cried buckets the day he left. His last words, after rumpling my long curly hair, were, "Better stop dyeing it, or it'll fall out."

"I don't dye it. I tint it."

He'd widened his eyes in mock horror. "My little baby sister dyes her hair!" And then he was gone.

Yeah, I do tint it. I have the complexion of a redhead, just like my mom, but my hair is darker.

The last thing that happened before my sixteenth birthday, a month later, was that I decided to be a doctor. I don't know exactly what happened, but I'd stopped at the hospital to get a lift home from Dad and had had to wait downstairs. I saw patients being admitted, and patients being discharged. Whap! It hit me. They come in sick, and go out well. Most of them do, anyway; I'm not a romantic. I know people die, but sometimes a doctor makes a difference.

My dad was shocked when I asked for the book *Gray's Anatomy* for my sixteenth birthday. Turns out he thought I was only interested in the graphics of male anatomy. We'd been sitting in his study, and he'd mumbled his way through "Thebirdsandthebees" and "Thefactsoflife." Honestly. A man, a doctor of forty-five, and he was blushing!

I got hysterical. Through my giggles, I explained my decision.

He'd looked at me in relief at first, then said in disbelief, "You? I mean you do?"

"Yeah, me," I'd answered. "Why not? Can't I follow in your footsteps? Just because Tim doesn't want to, does that mean I can't join your club? I thought you weren't a chauvinist. Wait till I tell Mom!" I did wait, one minute to enjoy his expression, then yelled, "Mom! Mom! Dad says I can't be a doctor!"

He'd started laughing then. His glasses slid down his nose, he ran his hands through his salt-and-pepper hair, and tears were running down his face. At that moment, Mom hit the door of the study. For some reason, she'd thought Dad had slapped me and was crying about it. That got me even more hysterical; my dad is not the physical type.

My trip down memory lane was canceled when the traffic cleared up past the exit and I had to concentrate on keeping the bug on the road. It shimmied and swayed as if wanting to go where the winds went, and I felt battered as I turned into the hospital's parking lot at last.

Sharp, stinging rain struck me as I ran across the lot. It was only three in the afternoon, but pitch black and I could hear the wail of an ambulance already.

I wasn't supposed to be on duty that day, and although the Teen Volunteers' esteemed head, Mrs. Nettles, is usually a stickler for rules, she was glad to see me. "Teresa! Teresa Murphy. How brave of you to come. There are only a few of you here."

"It's Tessa," I corrected gently, joining her at the entrance to the tiny office she shares with the head of the Pink Ladies, Mrs. Clark.

"Tessa, of course. Forgive me." Mrs. Nettles looked harassed, but each hair on her lovely blond head was in place. She straightened her back, which thrust forth the large shoulder pads of a designer jacket, giving her the look of a misplaced football player.

"A smock first." She stepped into her office and took one of the aqua, clean but shapeless garments out of a locker. They were always too big for my small build, and could have used some nips, tucks, and large shoulder pads, too. I put the smock on over my white cotton T-shirt as she checked out my white ducks and sneaks. "It's wonderful you're always so clean."

I didn't admit to having bought two pairs of new ducks and sneaks, plus several plain T's before joining the "bedpan brigade" a week before. Mrs. Nettles stashed my small shoulder bag, after I'd taken out a few dollars, my compact and lipstick, and my name tag. The first three items went into my pockets, and the fourth was being pinned on as she locked my bag up in the locker. This little routine, which had been perfected by Mrs. Nettles, did make things easier on us kids. I knew in other hospitals, in other parts of the country, they still made girls wear pink-striped pinafores—gross—and the boys got to wear smocks. This way we were much more equal.

"Now, what can I do?" I asked.

Mrs. Nettles checked the schedule lying on her desk. "Go up to the third floor and help Maxwell Mitchell set up cots in the doctors' and nurses' lounges. Then we'll see."

I nodded and hurried away. Maxwell Mitchell. My brain said ho hum, but my heart went rat-a-tat. I'm just like anyone else; I can fall for a charmer. But not him. He has blue-green eyes, coal-black hair, a dimple in his chin, and half the girls wear his heart on their sleeves. Too much competition, and he came on to me too much. I always figured if I tumbled, he'd love and leave. I had that experience once. Once is plenty.

The elevators were jam-packed, so I took to the stairs, hearing the storm in the stairwell. The lights were flickering, and I hurried, even though I knew the hospital had its own generator for emergencies. If the whole of Texas were blacked out, we'd still have power for days.

I was breathless and hot when I arrived at the doctors' lounge and found Max struggling with an army cot. Being an ex-Girl Scout, and a sometime camper, can bring expertise in the weirdest areas. "Hi," I said brightly and hit the right notches to help him stretch the awkward thing out.

"I'm impressed." Max grinned. White teeth can be blinding.

"Wow, great!" I answered. "I mean, I exist only to impress you."

"Has anyone ever told you you're sarcastic?" His smile dimmed, but only by a few watts.

I got another cot from the pile stacked up against the wall, saying, "Sure, it's one of my charms." I set it up in the blink of an eye, but my audience did not applaud. He must have taken notes though, for the next one went up almost as fast. From then on, it was a competition. We moved to the nurses' lounge and continued the battle, ending in a tie.

As we were making up the cots, I considered starting a pillow fight, but then he said, "Okay, you finish up here, and I'll run down to see what's next. Back in a flash."

I figured he was trying to make himself points with Mrs. Nettles, and yelled after him, "I'll be in the playroom, see you later."

The elevator doors were closing as I heard him say, "It'll be your pleasure."

Grrr. Those last sheets and blankets hung off the cots as though the hurricane had put them there, but I didn't care. Let Max straighten them out; I headed for pediatrics.

The ambulatory kids were all gathered in the playroom. Some kept trying to peek through the cheerful curtains that covered the windows, but most of them were scared. One toddler, a two-year-old thumb sucker, came over to me with tearstained eyes and outstretched arms. I lifted her up and carried her over to Ms. Renfrew, the head pediatrics nurse.

"Oh, Tessa, thank goodness." She had mussy brown hair poking out of her peaked white hat. "I'm all alone here and I have to check on the bedders. Will you watch the little angels? Read to them or something?"

"Sure." Bedders was her name for the bedridden, and she bustled off, leaving me with a horde of devils, not angels. However, as a new face, I got their attention and gathered them in the middle of the room.

I was trying to put some enthusiasm into a rather mediocre story they all seemed to love, when Ms. Renfrew came back tugging the front end of a bed. Max was pushing it, and the kid riding on it was yelling, "Faster, faster."

"We're moving everyone in here," Ms. Renfrew told me. "I'll take over here if you'll help Max." She hugged me; she hugs practically everyone. "Thank you, Tessa."

Doomed again. As Max and I went down the hall, he put an arm around me. "Cut it out," I said, stepping on his foot.

"Ms. Renfrew says no one gets enough affection, so I thought I'd give you some."

"Sarcastic people don't deserve affection," I zapped him.

"Maybe if they got more they wouldn't be sarcastic."

"Some of us are beyond saving."

We kept up the banter while pushing the beds, all five of them, into the playroom. The kids loved it. Max and I were both sweating now; the air was so humid I felt like an overcooked spaghetti squash.

Then Ms. Renfrew informed us that we had to go up to med, the medical floor, to put up more cots. The local nursing homes were being evacuated, but the patients couldn't be transported to Houston in time.

When Max punched the elevator button, I said, "Oh, you're so lazy—it's only one floor," and headed for the stairwell.

Wrong choice. I was a few steps up when the lights went out. "Tessa," Max said in a low, sexy voice. "Alone at last."

"Get your hands offa me!" I yelled as the hospital generator took over and the lights came back on.

"Tessa! Is something wrong?" Jordan Franklin was on the landing above us. Sigh. Jordan was tall, blond, gray-eyed, and cute in a serious way. I was full of illusions and thought that med students should be serious; healers and all that. Besides, he was serving a proctorship with my dad and I thought that made him perfect for me. The two of us shoulder to shoulder... "Tessa?" he asked. "Are you all right?"

I glared at Max. "No, yes, I mean, we were just fooling around."

Oooh, was that the worst thing to say. Jordan frowned. "This isn't the time to be fooling around. Those cots have to be put up."

"Right." I hurried past him. All the time Max and I were setting up cots, I thought about Jordan. Okay, I admitted to myself, sometimes he sounded more than serious, like stuffy. But he was older—twenty-one—and so brilliant he'd be going into his second year of medical school in the fall. By the time he was interning, I'd be in premed. Then he'd take *me* seriously, and I'd get him to lighten up. Perfect.

The cots were rollaways this time, and there were more frames than mattresses. Max was going to go downstairs for them, when the elevator doors opened up and a gurney was shoved onto the floor by a burly aide. "This all you got?" he complained. Yeah, we did look like a disaster area, but go hang chintz in an emergency.

A floor nurse, Gail Robbins, one of the nicest and youngest in the hospital, said, "We've got one private. What's the problem?"

"Possible concussion. Fallen tree. Bad smack." The aide wasn't one to mince words.

I looked with curiosity at the first victim of Aaron that I'd seen. She had a bandage on her temple, a hugely swollen black eye, and a trickle of dried blood on her cheek. A slim white hand, ringless, was resting against the sheet. The other one was pressed into her cheek as though keeping her good eye closed. I felt so sorry for her. The blood meant that emergency had been too busy to clean her up. Dad must be there by now, I thought abstractedly, still looking at the patient. His office was across the compound, and he'd never think of deserting as so many of the other doctors had done.

"Okay," Ms. Robbins said. "Put her in the private, 4A-4. If she's all right and we get busy and need the room, we'll move her later."

We did get busy, but most of the patients were ambulatory, if elderly and unsteady. Max bedded them down, and I was searching for more blankets in the utility closet near 4A-4 when I heard the screams.

True to my training, I looked out in the hall for a doctor, a nurse or anyone with more knowledge than I. Nope, there were patients roaming, disoriented, but no white uniforms.

The screams called me into the room. The hall light cast a long shadow of the patient sitting up in bed. "Turn on the bloody light," she said.

I flipped the wall switch and her bedside lamp went on. "Why doesn't anyone answer this buzzer?" She had been clutching the cord with a finger pressed down on the button, but released it now that I was there. I started to explain about the hospital being shorthanded, but then she spied the phone beside the lamp. Grabbing the receiver, she listened for a second, then complained, "Doesn't anything work around here?"

"We have to tell them downstairs that you want it connected. Please, don't get excited, you may have a concussion." I put on a very calm tone, but inside I was shaken. There was something so odd about her. When I'd seen her out in the hall, both eyes had been shut, but now the unswollen one was open. It was a brilliant green. The black, swollen eye showed a slit of green so I knew the eyes matched, ha, but her skin was as pale as the bandage on her forehead. The streak of dried blood that had bothered me before gave her the look of Frankenstein's bride.

"I'll get something to clean you up," I said, going into the bathroom and wetting a cloth with cool water. While I was taking a swipe at the blood with my right hand, my left was feeling the temperature of her skin. If she was clammy or hot, I'd run for help, but she seemed normal.

And her reflexes were fine as she thrust both my hands away, demanding, "Is there a pay phone?"

"Yes, but you can't go there. It's too far away." Her good eye welled up with tears. I patted her wispy beige hair and said lamely, "Maybe I could make the call for you?"

"Would you? It's 4..."

"Wait a minute." I opened the drawer of the bedside table and found the tiny pink pencil and loud pink stationery the Pink Ladies provided. "Shoot."

She winced at that word, and mumbled the area code. Again, I heard 4, but didn't get the rest. Then she went on, "555-9145. Tell Todd that Stacy is in... What's the name of this hospital?"

"Community General in Lake Watson." I had the number down, and I scribbled Todd and Stacy. When I looked up, her good eye was staring at me.

"Lake Watson." She sighed. "I thought I got farther than that."

"Pardon me?"

Suddenly she proved her reflexes were fine again. This time by grabbing the pink paper and asking loudly, "Who are you?"

"Me? I'm a TeeVee. Uh, Teen Volunteer." I couldn't imagine what was wrong now.

She shook her bandaged head. "How do I know that? I can't trust anyone." I was going to protest, then she got even louder. "He sent you, didn't he? Go away! Now!"

"Look, I'm sorry." I backed to the door. I didn't want any hassle; Mrs. Nettles can be awfully strict. But I gave it one last try. "Please, I'd like to help you. Really. You seem to be in trouble."

"I bet you know all about it."

I shook my head. She was trembling and it scared me. I fled out into the hall and stopped the first nurse I saw, Ms. Robbins. I gasped, "The patient in 4A-4. You'd better check on her."

"Did you find those blankets?" Ms. Robbins asked, then seeing my empty hands added, "Try the closet near 4A-10. And don't worry, Tessa, I'll see what the problem is."

That was all I could do. Except get the blankets and go back to work. That was tough enough. More senior citizens were needing attention by then, and what with keeping them calm, giving them tea and juice, I was more than busy. Funny, I was soaked through with the humid heat, but the elders complained that they were freezing, and their tea wasn't hot enough.

I bummed a couple of bobby pins at the nurses' station, made a pit stop in the john, replaited my single braid and secured it on top of my head. Cold, wet paper towels on my face reminded me of the troubled Stacy. Should I have done something else?

"Like what, Murphy?" I asked my mirror image, then noticed that whatever makeup I'd had on had taken a long hike. I took the compact and lipstick out of my pocket and used them sparingly. The excitement, work or heat had put a natural bloom on my cheeks, and I didn't break the mirror, so I figured I was okay.

Refreshed anyway, I found Max waiting for me by the nurses' station. It was quiet. I couldn't hear the wind or rain or anything that I'd been hearing constantly for hours. "Is it over?" I asked Max.

"No, silly, it's the eye of the storm."

"Oh."

"Hey," Max said softly. "I didn't mean to call you silly. I know you're not used to this, and you've been great, really great. But it's not over, more than likely we'll have worse coming up."

"Oh," I said again, feeling sillier than silly.

"Anyway, you're wanted down in emergency."

"Oh." *The silliest!*

Angry at myself for my lack of vocabulary, I took to the stairs again. Max had seemed so sweet that my stupid, and silly, little heart fluttered. The staircase was dimmer than before; either the generator was losing power or it wasn't wasted there.

I rounded the corner of the third floor and ran smack-dab into a very tall figure wearing operating greens. "Sorry," I said up to the face that was half-covered with a standard mask. How could he breathe?

"You work here?" The mask sucked in and out.

"Yeah," I answered, taken aback. Then I remembered that he probably wasn't on staff and wouldn't know the familiar aqua smocks. I pointed to my identity tag. Above my name it had the logo of Community General, and the words Teen Volunteer. "I'm a TeeVee," I choked out.

"Fine. Then you can tell me where a patient of mine is. She was brought in with a head injury."

I tried to see what his face looked like under the mask, but all that was visible were kind of fat eyes. Baggy, I mean. Lots of lids and lots of bulges underneath. And sparse eyebrows. I couldn't even tell what color anything was.

"I asked you a question."

Whew, he was right on top of me almost. I'm only five-four, and he was at least a foot taller. Get rid of him! That's all I could think about. "Head injury? Uh, uh, uh, you mean a woman? Called Stacy?"

He got closer. "That's right. Where is she?"

Go say no to someone like that! "Uh, room 4A-4."

He didn't even say thank-you. When I'm a doctor, I thought, I'll be more polite. Especially to TeeVees. And I wouldn't scare them. "I should have kicked him," I muttered aloud, my fear gone and my anger rising.

In emergency it was my dad who wanted to see me, and he got the flash of that anger. "Dad, I was busy upstairs."

"Tessa, we will have coffee and talk for a few minutes." Dad put on his professorial look. "Your mother called, and she's sure you're overworked and on the verge of collapse. If I don't reassure her soon, she'll ride the hurricane over here on her Magic Brush, capture you and I'll never see you again."

I giggled helplessly. Mom's "Magic Brush" was the one she used to lay in large, flat washes on her watercolors. We'd been giving it imaginary powers since I was a child.

"I'm serious," Dad went on. "She'll take you to the land of cerulean and cerise druids, and I'll be stuck roaming these stark white halls forever calling, Tessa! Tessa!"

"No, no! I can't stand it!" I clutched my heart. "Those are the rude druids. I'll phone her, I promise."

"First, my little teacup, we'll have some food. 'Cause she'll ask if you've eaten."

Too true. The coffee shop was closed for lack of help, and Dad didn't want to go to the basement cafeteria because the intercom system was acting puny; he wanted to be near emergency. So, fifteen minutes later, after sandwiches from a machine and coffee and doughnuts from a Salvation Army uniform, we sat in the lobby catching up. He was hyper, telling funny stories and making the trials and tribulations of emergency sound like a lark. I was laughing at him when Jordan Franklin rushed up.

Jordan looked immaculate, as always, as though perspiration wouldn't dare attack such a prince, but he was flustered. "Dr. Murphy, STAT! That patient with the head injury—that young woman? She's lapsed into a coma!"

Chapter Two

I almost spilled what was left of my coffee. My father was already up and running when I yelled, "Dad! I saw her. She was okay and there was a doctor on the stairs..."

"Call Fiona, Tessa." He hadn't heard me.

Anyway, I watched while Dad and Jordan commandeered an elevator, then I headed for Mrs. Nettles's office like a good daughter, although my mind was with Stacy.

I used the phone and told Mom I was fine, and no, I wasn't working too hard, and no, I wasn't tired, and yes, I'd seen Dad, and no, he wasn't tired, and yes, we'd both eaten. Them druids weren't gonna get me, no how.

Mrs. Nettles hovered over me while I was on the phone and, sure enough, I had to reassure her, too. Since she had eavesdropped on my end of the conversation, she should have been convinced. Not her. "I

The Eye of the Storm

have to get back upstairs," I said, dodging her questions.

At the door to the stairwell I stopped, turned back and went to the elevators. Was I scared of those stairs, of another too close encounter? Well, a tiny bit.

An elevator came, several people took their time getting out, then I got in with some patients and that same burly aide who'd brought Stacy up. I pushed the fourth-floor button and then remembered about that phone number Stacy had given me. I remembered about it, but not it, except that the area code she hadn't finished had begun with four, and that there was a four somewhere in it. Blast! Why couldn't I remember it?

"What's the matter, cutie?" the aide asked me. I was leaning against the elevator wall as the doors opened on two, and my face was all scrunched up trying to visualize the number again. I glanced at the aide. He was Mexican, middle-aged, and I thought his name was Rudy. I saw in that glance that he wasn't coming on to me, he was acting more fatherly than anything. "You okay?"

"Oh, sure." I managed a smile. "It's just, you know that patient you brought up to four before, the one with the possible concussion? She's in a coma now."

"Wha'?" His heavy eyebrows shot up in surprise. "You sure? She okay before." The elevator was now traveling slowly again.

I nodded as the doors opened on three. Now I recalled why I always used the stairs; the elevators took forever. "Did she talk to you at all?"

"Nah. She seemed like she was, you know, scared of me."

"Yeah, me too." Finally we were on four.

"Hey!" Rudy pressed the open button and stopped me when I was halfway across the foyer. "Don' worry 'bout it too much. These things, they happen, you know?"

I waved at him. "Right."

I hurried to 4A-4. I was too late. Ms. Robbins was already making up the empty bed with fresh sheets. "I'll do that." I took the bottom sheet and whipped it into place. "How is she? The patient? She didn't, er, she didn't..."

"No darling, she didn't die." Ms. Robbins tucked in the corner nearest her, then came around the bed. "Your dad and what's his name took her down to X ray by the back elevator."

"Oh. Ms. Robbins, did she say anything to you when you checked on her?"

Ms. Robbins stood back and watched me work. "You surely do good corners, and it's time to start calling me Gail, especially after tonight. You're doing real well."

I stopped midcorner and looked at her, pleased with the compliment. She wasn't all that much older than me, but most of the nurses were sticklers about the formalities. Gail had an open, caring familiarity about her with the patients, and I liked her enormously. Her black Afro was sticking to her head now, and I could see almost black circles under her deep brown eyes. Her skin was covered with sweat, too. "Are you okay?" I asked.

"I've been better." She smiled. "It's been a long night, and it's going to get longer. I don't know what we'd do without you kids. Anyway, what did you ask me?"

I repeated the question as I finished the last corner and reached for the lightweight blanket that was hanging on the chair.

The Eye of the Storm

"Oh, no, not much. Except she accused me of spying on her or some such rot. She was terribly frightened of something."

"You didn't happen to see a strange doctor up here wearing operating greens and a surgical mask, did you?"

Gail thought a moment, and while she was doing that she sat down in the chair. I could see her legs were slightly swollen and wondered about that. She said, "Yes, matter of fact I did. Haven't seen too many doctors tonight, and I thought it was weird that he was in greens up here. But then I figured he'd popped up from surgery to see another patient of his."

"Did he come into this room at all?"

"Ah, dear." Gail shut her eyes for a second. "I just don't know. Is it important?"

Now I was really concerned about her. She was a small woman, smaller even than me, and now she was looking very frail. "No, it doesn't matter at all." I walked over to the chair, peered down and felt her forehead. It was a little clammy, but not overly warm. "Gail, your legs are swollen, and I know you're not feeling well. Do you have high blood pressure?"

Gail laughed. "Tessa, if you're going to be a doctor, you'd better come up with the other reason for swollen legs—besides, of course, the fact that I've been on them since six this morning."

I stalled, checking my watch. Cripes, it was already nine o'clock. I'd been in the hospital myself for six hours, and the wind had resumed howling outside. The eye had passed, and I hadn't noticed it. "Nineteen hours is a long time... er, are you pregnant?"

"Right on!" Gail laughed. "Maybe you will make a good doctor after all."

"You're darn tooting I will." I laughed with her. By the time I'd persuaded her to take a nap on the bed that I'd just made up, and promised her I would wake her if any crisis patients came in, I'd forgotten all about Stacy.

Then I had to get back on the job. We got so busy, I worked like a robot, part of me concentrating on what I was doing while the other wondered about what I didn't know and how fast I could learn.

It was getting quieter outside. The storm had to be passing. My watch now said it was one-thirty in the morning. Where had all that time gone?

I saw Max again by the nurses' station. I hadn't paid much attention to him all night, except noticing occasionally, when we were working side by side, that he was very efficient. Now I could see his fabulous eyes were at half-mast, and one of his hands was clutching the desk as though it was a life preserver.

"Hey," I said softly, walking over to him. "Why don't you take a nap?"

"Tessa," he muttered, half-asleep on his feet. "Why do you hate me?"

"I don't hate you," I said, flustered. "I, I, look, I heard they've got cots set up in the kitchen. Go take a nap."

"You mean someone took our jobs away from us? That there's some place in this hospital that has cots that we didn't set up? How cruel."

"Oh boy, are you tired." I diagnosed his condition without having to look at a medical dictionary. The poor thing was having trouble standing upright; how could I not take pity on him? I'm such a humanitarian, I lent him my shoulder and started walking him to the elevators.

The Eye of the Storm 27

"That's the first time you've ever been nice to me," he said when we got to the wall. He leaned on it and me at the same time, putting his hand in the big chrome ashtray there. It was filled with sand and butts. "Ah, sand feels good. Nice here at the beach, isn't it?"

"Max." I lifted his hand out of the ashtray and brushed it off. It was large, warm and tanned. I dropped the hand like I'd been burned; I mean, why would I want to hold on to it suddenly? The arm swung in a detached way and I knew Max needed more than a nap—like maybe twenty-four hours in the sack. I punched the elevator button again. Elevators, I concluded, are like cops: they're never there in a dangerous situation.

"You don't hate me?" Max was really rambling. And he'd rambled back to where I'd rather he hadn't.

"I don't hate anyone," I punted.

Whew, an elevator came. I shoved Max in, pushing the ground-floor button. The doors closed as he was saying, "You're so pretty and you hate me."

Whoa! I almost banged on the doors to bring him back. Who wouldn't want to hear that again? I mean, I know I'm pretty sometimes, when I'm all dressed up and made up, but then I look at my mother and fade away to average.

Had to be hallucinations from exhaustion, I decided, remembering what he'd said earlier about it being my pleasure to see him again. Remembering also the snide remarks we'd exchanged. So, I went on my merry way. *Merry?* No way. After about fifteen minutes, I'd forgotten everything again.

The patients who could walk were sent down to the cafeteria to make room for the new ones coming up from emergency. Even though Aaron had almost left us, he was still leaving behind casualties. His victims, really. I'd never seen anything so devastating, except, I guess, on television, but there had been a screen between me and the devastation. I couldn't help thinking about the possibility of nuclear war, and how it would be three million times worse than what I was seeing.

By four in the morning, Aaron was truly gone and there were ten cots set up by the nurses' station between wings A and B. Most of the patients were either crying or whimpering now. Their houses, their personal possessions were all gone. One woman's son was still in emergency; another had lost her dog. They comforted each other as best they could.

Struck by that scene, I tried to call Mom from the nurses' station, but the lines were down. That made me tense, all right. Now I understood Dad—the way he'd disappeared from time to time, the way he hadn't been able to make it to some parent-teacher thing, or once when I'd been in a school play. And why he'd usually been asleep when I had something important to tell him.

But most of all, why he'd decided to stop pretending to be a family practitioner and become one. He'd always made house calls when his colleagues had not, and had even been called "Saint John." So, instead of discouraging me in my chosen profession, Aaron actually did me a favor. He took the stardust out of my eyes, and showed me how important a hand to a patient was. Of course I had no plans to become "Saint Tessa," but I knew I could become a dedicated, caring doctor.

Chapter Three

After all that self-examination, I got my come-uppance. Gail woke up and booted me off the floor for some R & R. Rest and recuperation. She assured me, without a put-down, that, "Your patients will be here when you get back."

My patients! I loved the sound of that, and went without a fight. But I only got as far as the third floor. I couldn't resist popping in on pediatrics to see if Ms. Renfrew and the children were all right.

Most of the parents of the already hospitalized kids were in the playroom by then. It looked like a party: ice cream, Coke, tea, coffee and coffee cakes sent up from the cafeteria.

The hall was another story. It was jam-packed with kids in cots, both rollaways and army. The rooms were stuffed with kids in beds and also on floor mats. There were some fresh nurses tending to Aaron's injured, but still Ms. Renfrew was glad to see me. She was so glad to see me that I got the job of going around to soothe the kids who weren't asleep. I took it, not admitting that I was supposed to be on R & R.

It was hushed; children who are hurt don't make much noise. I'd just gotten a four-year-old to sleep when Max showed up.

"Hi," he said softly, leaning over the slats on the other side of the bed. "Poor baby. Is she okay?" He tugged the sheet over her and tucked her in. One of his large fingers stroked her cheek, and she moved in sleep to hold it. "Wish I had a teddy bear or something."

"There are some stuffed toys in the playroom," I said gruffly. The sight of his kindness touched me, and I hurried away, coming back a few minutes later with a floppy rabbit. The child was still holding his finger. As far as I could see, he hadn't made a move to get away.

Max removed his finger carefully, and replaced it with the bunny's ear. It was a tender scene, but for some reason I got angry about it. I wanted to hold on to my image of Max as macho-man; I didn't want to feel what I was feeling toward him. He looked up. "Tessa, your eyes are like burnt holes in a blanket. Why don't you hie yourself down to the kitchen and take a nap too?"

"Burnt holes in a blanket?" I'd never heard the expression before, and of course wanted a mirror immediately.

"My grandfather always said that when one of the little ones looked tired. I've got six brothers and sisters, you know."

We had been whispering above the child, but my "No" sounded out loudly. We moved away from the bed, toward the nurses' station. "I didn't know." The only fact I knew about him was that he'd been in Lake

The Eye of the Storm 31

Watson most of his life. I'd heard some girls, once, in the locker room after gym class, talking about him and what a hunk he was. One of the girls said she'd heard he'd been born in Oklahoma. "Seven kids, huh? Must be nice, I only have a brother, but speaking of families, I've gotta go downstairs and talk to my father. I tried to call my mother but the lines are down. I really have to go."

"Get some rest, too." He followed me to the stairs and held open the door for me.

"Yeah," I said over my shoulder, speeding my feet down the stairs as if he were chasing me. Nothing had been said again about my being pretty, but he'd looked at me that way, and he'd been so nice to that little girl. Six brothers and sisters? Then, of course, he'd know how to treat children. It didn't make him special at all, did it?

Those stairs had been unlucky for me all night, and nothing changed. There was a tall man coming up, and he was wearing greens. He wasn't wearing a mask, but still it took me a very frightened moment to realize the man was only Jordan Franklin.

"Tessa, you're still here?" He frowned.

"Yeah, sure, why not?" I asked. I hadn't been expecting a medal, but I surely could have used some appreciation.

He cleared his throat as if to make a speech and sure enough he did. "I should think that someone your age would have been dismissed long ago. Perhaps I should speak to Mrs. Nettles on your behalf."

"Don't do me any favors, Jordan," I snapped and then was amazed at myself. I had known I was all at odds with myself because of the hurricane, the patients and their injuries, plus my confusion over Max, but what had happened to the old me who used to fawn over Jordan? I went on, "I'm here because I want to be here. Why don't you go home?"

"Me? Why, your father needs me."

"Tut, tut, Jordan. The hospital needs you, as it needs me. I'm sure that you've been very important tonight, but so have I." I was backing away now, my speedy sneaks not so speedily retreating. I felt the door of the first floor press against my back. Suddenly I was so tired, I could barely move. Feeling like a goose, I stared up at him, standing some stairs above me.

Jordan must have noticed my condition and tried to make amends. "Of course, you're right. I don't know what we'd have done tonight without you, er, helpers."

My face was flushed now. "You mean the little people, don't you?" I leaned against the door, opening it.

"No, I don't mean that at all. Look, I'm sorry."

"Forget it, just forget it," I said, escaping. Crossing the lobby was like swimming through deep pudding. I smelled coffee; the luncheonette had opened, but I couldn't get to it. The first slick, beige chair I came to swallowed me up and my eyes closed gratefully.

Someone must have told my father that his little girl was out there asleep, because that was how he acted when he came to wake me. "Tessa, Tessa, I think maybe you'd better go home now. Tessa. You're all tuckered out. Let me see if I can get Jordan to drive you."

"No!" I sat bolt upright, wide awake now.

"What? I thought you liked Jordan," he teased, and I wondered how obvious I'd been all those nights that Jordan had decorated our dining-room table.

"Dad."

"Okay, okay." He smiled. "Now, will you go home?"

"No. Aren't you the one who keeps telling me how hard interning is? That an intern has to be up and ready for anything for twenty-four hours at a time? Well, I'm getting some early training."

Dad smiled even more broadly, and I thought I saw—no, I did see that he was proud of me for not giving in. "So, how about joining your old man for breakfast then, and we'll talk some more about it."

There was nothing he could do or say that would make me leave the hospital. We plowed through some scrambled eggs, bacon and waffles, drowning it all with coffee, and I agreed to take a nap downstairs before going about my regular Thursday duties. It was hard to believe that it was only Thursday; Aaron had seemed to cover about five days instead of one.

The luncheonette was filling up, and some customers eyed our booth suggestively, but we ordered more coffee. "I wonder who decorated this place," I said, looking around. It was crammed to the hilt with plastic: chairs, tables, the counter, the booths, and even silly-looking dusty plastic flowers stuck into plastic vases.

The coffee came in plastic mugs, too. Dad sipped his. "We could have gone to the cafeteria, but it's full of cots. Wait until you see it."

"By the way, speaking of patients, how's that Stacy?"

"Stacy?" Dad looked blank.

"The one with the head injury who lapsed into a coma. You know, she was up on the med floor."

"Oh, her. Where'd you get the name Stacy? She came in as a Jane Doe." He was full of curiosity. "She wouldn't give her name, her address, or anything."

"Tell me how she is, and I'll tell you how I know."

"Sometimes you are exactly like your mother." Dad said it like a compliment; I took it as one. "Okay, okay, she had a subdural hematoma that she didn't have when she was first X-rayed. It was one of the most peculiar things last night. The only thing we could figure is she got injured again, after the first X ray."

"Injured again?" My voice went up. All I could think about was her fear and the man on the stairs. "How?"

"Sssh." Dad glanced around, then leaned forward. "This sort of thing happens, but we don't like to broadcast it." I was anxious for him to go on, and nodded. "I, er, we think, maybe, she could have been dropped in transit from emergency to med."

"Dropped?" I whispered. "You mean like off the gurney?"

"It happens in the best of hospitals, especially during times like last night when everything is hurry, hurry."

"No." I shook my head. "No way. I saw her when she was brought up. Rudy brought her, and I talked to her afterward."

"You did?" Dad's glasses slipped down his nose again. His gesture of nervously pushing them back up was as familiar to me as the long nose on his face. "Rudy, huh? He's one of the best."

"Exactly." We were still talking quietly, but I put a lot of emphasis on that word. "When I talked to her, she was fine. No fever. She wasn't clammy, and her reflexes were okay. She was very agitated." I went on to explain the rest of it. The phone number, how I knew her name was Stacy, and the doctor on the stairs. My tiredness hit me again and I yawned, then stumbled on. "Maybe he did something to her, like hitting her."

The Eye of the Storm

"Tessa, there have been a few strange doctors around here, but I doubt if any of them have hit their patients."

Grrr. One minute he'd treated me like a colleague, and the next he was being condescending. "But Dad, she said to me, 'He sent you, didn't he?' and she was so scared. The phone call was so important to her."

"Do you remember the number? Someone should be notified about her condition."

"No, I've been trying, but with all that's been happening, well, you know."

"Sure," Dad said gently, then thumped his head with the palm of his hand. "I've got it. I bet she tried to get out of bed to make the stupid call, then fell and hurt her head."

"So, how did she get back into bed?" I asked with what I thought was supreme logic.

Dad pondered that for a moment, then said, "Anyone could have put her back. A nurse's aide or one of you kids who didn't know enough to check on her vital signs."

"Thanks a lot!" I was ready to scream. "There were no nurse's aides up there last night, and we kids, as you put it, know better." I was ready to swear, but one doesn't swear around one's father. At least not me around mine. "Besides, I got Gail to check on her after I saw her and she was fine. Paranoid, but fine. She accused Gail of spying on her or something."

"Gail?" Dad pushed his glasses into place again. "You mean Gail Robbins?"

"She asked me to call her Gail," I said in a small voice.

"She shouldn't have." He finished his coffee. "I've got to get back. Tessa, you've shown remarkable fortitude tonight, and I'm glad about that. However, you must understand that informality has no place in a hospital situation. It is quite appropriate for Ms. Robbins to call you by your first name. But it is totally inappropriate for you to call her Gail. Do you understand?"

"Yeah, but anyway, she saw the doctor, too. And it was after that Stacy went into a coma. Ask her, *Ms. Robbins*, about it, okay?"

"I will. Of course, in the meantime, if you remember that number, please let me know."

By then he was standing, bringing out bills from his wallet to pay for our breakfast. "Sure," I said, not meaning it much.

He leaned over and kissed me on the cheek, then loped off. I saw a nurse smile bewitchingly at him, and then saw a civilian fluff up her blue hair. Yep, my dad could have been a real lady-killer except for my mom who is unpredictable, flighty, and loves him passionately.

I drooped my head over the dregs of my coffee, thinking about the conversation. Sometimes Dad is so much fun, but then, as quick as a tic, he gets on what I call his "Hypocratic Oath" kick. All serious; no humor. And when he's on that kick, there isn't much room for speculation. I was sure he'd decided that Stacy had injured herself, and that I'd fantasized the fear I'd felt with the strange doctor in the stairwell.

I wished with all my might that I could talk to Tim.

My nap was enough to keep me going until five in the afternoon when my shift ended. The hospital seemed almost normal by then. The uninjured evacuees had left, along with the slightly hurt. The lines had been repaired, and I called Mom to let her know I'd be home eventually.

And lucky me. Max and I got to take down the cots. He was suspiciously quiet. Almost grumpy. I thought perhaps he'd remembered calling me pretty and regretted it. The memory of the child, his finger and the rabbit kept intruding on my brain until I called myself a dumb bunny, and told myself to stuff it. No pun intended.

Mrs. Nettles bustled onto the floor at the end of our shift. She'd gone home and changed into another outfit with gigantic shoulder pads, and she announced that we, Max and I, could leave. She made us sound like a couple.

So did he. "Tessa, baby, could you drop me at the M & G Diner off the Houston Interchange?"

"Baby?" I croaked. "Hey, in case you don't know, I've got a father. And he hasn't called me baby since I kicked him in the knee for it when I was ten."

"Whoops, sorry." Max grinned. He'd gotten to me and he knew it. "I'd better get some knee pads."

"Make sure they're as thick as your head," I retorted, going for the stairwell. I figured that all that could possibly happen to me on those stairs had already happened. Max followed me, crooning, "Oh, please, Tessa. Please give me a lift. I'll never call you baby again."

On the first floor, I turned and said savagely, "How about promising you'll never talk to me again, huh?"

"Sure."

"Okay, it's the blue Volks bug out in the parking lot. I'll be right there, but I have to talk to my father first."

He winked and went without a word.

I found Dad leaning over an empty gurney in emergency. He was half-asleep. "Hey, why don't you climb in. Take a nap."

"I've been thinking about it." He looked down at me. "Oh, haven't I seen you somewhere before?"

"Nope, never met before in all our lives."

Dad's glasses had been on top of his head. Once he put them on correctly, he seemed almost awake. "Ah, yes. I knew I'd seen you before. Didn't you used to be smaller?"

"Dad, Pop, Father mine, how about going home? I got told to leave, maybe I should do you the same favor."

"Can't yet." He rubbed his head until his salt-and-pepper hair stood up. "Most of the doctors are back, but they need to be filled in on the patients. I 'spect I won't get out of here for another couple of hours."

"Yeah, okay. I wanted to ask you about that Stacy patient. What's happening?"

"Oh." Dad massaged his head some more, managing to get his hair flattened out into patches of neatness. "Dr. Jessup is going to operate around six. Blood clot on the brain. Oh, I told you that."

"Yeah, but the last time you gave me the professional courtesy of calling it a subdural hematoma." I saw him smile, then asked, "Did she regain consciousness?"

"No, and I saw Ms. Robbins. You were right. Agitated but awake and strong."

"Yeah, well, did she tell you about seeing the doctor?"

"I didn't ask her about that." Dad wasn't giving an inch. No doctor likes to accuse another one of doing something fishy.

Before I let loose with something nasty, I buzzed him on the cheek and managed, "See you later."

I wasn't exactly in the best of moods approaching my car, and seeing Max draped over it did not improve my state of mind. Dad could be so exasperating at times. And why wouldn't he trust me? His own daughter?

"This is one ugly car," Max announced when I'd gotten close to the bug.

"Funny, it's always spoken highly of you," I said, unlocking the door. "What do you drive—a Rolls?"

"Ha," he said, getting into the front seat. Once he'd settled himself into the bucket, he reached immediately for the seat belt. Was that a slur on my driving, I wondered, or merely a regard for the law?

"Well what, then?" I started the car, shifted impatiently and shot backward.

"A motorbike," he answered, watching me shift again, shoot to the entrance, brake, shift once more and turn. "My mother dropped me off last night, though. I figured the bike was safer at the house. You must have had a good teacher," he added, after I'd shifted once more. "Most girls couldn't drive a stick shift if their lives depended on it."

"I'm not most girls," I said. "Besides, I thought you promised not to talk."

"I lied," he said.

I knew I'd think of a scathing remark tomorrow, so I decided to ignore him. But when a few miles went by and he hadn't said a word, I sneaked a peek at him. He was sound asleep! Of all the nerve! First he bums a ride, then he talks when he'd promised not to, and then he falls asleep. With that kind of gall, he'd have his gall bladder out by the time he was thirty. I hoped.

When I pulled into the parking lot of the M & G Diner, I saw that it was closed. I said sweetly, "Hey, Max, if you want something to eat, you're out of luck."

He whipped his eyes open like a cat startled by a noise. A Siamese, perhaps, because of the color. "What?"

"It's closed." I actually smirked. "I suppose I could give you a lift home, maybe."

"I'd love that," he said, glancing at his watch. Then he searched in his pockets for something that turned out to be a key chain, with tons of keys rattling a tune of discord on it. "But I'm the one who has to open it up. My uncle's car got smacked by his garage during the storm, so he skipped breakfast and lunch, but dinner is as usual."

"Oh."

"Yeah." He unfastened his seat belt, stretched and yawned, the key ring clutched in his hand. "I've got to stick a dozen chickens on the grill, defrost the hamburgers, slice tomatoes, wash lettuce, let me see, oh, the lamb, it's the special tonight, and then set the tables..."

"You? I mean, you cook?" I sounded as if I were talking through a loudspeaker.

"Of course, don't you?" He was grinning like a Cheshire cat. Is there such a thing as a Cheshire-Siamese? That's what he looked like. "Anyway, the power wasn't off long enough to do much damage, I hope. And Uncle Dom has about thirty-five of those blue things in the freezer."

"Blue things?" I hadn't the foggiest idea what he was talking about.

"You know, those do-hickies that people take on picnics to keep things cold. I'd love to stay and chat, but

The Eye of the Storm 41

I've got to get going. Uncle Dom said the farmers delivered this morning, despite Aaron, but he only had time to stow the stuff away. I've got eggs waiting to be counted, milk to sniff and rhubarb pie to bake. You ought to stop by sometime; we're cheap, honest and home cooked. See you, Tessa, and thanks for the ride."

Honestly! I sat in the car watching him unlock the front door and had to slap my hands away from my seat belt. I wanted to watch macho-man bake rhubarb pies so much I could almost taste it. Or them.

Chapter Four

I kept mulling Max as a cook over in my mind while my mother fussed over me. Speaking of cooks, she's one of the great ones, and she'd whipped together her version of linguini with clam sauce as soon as I got home. Her version includes shrimp, scallops, more butter than oil, and lots of garlic. "Heaven, it's heaven, Mom."

"Good for you, too," she said. "Carbohydrates and protein. Have more."

She ladled a second helping into the bowl I was eating from; it's the only way to eat it, and I ate until I was full enough to burst. I pushed the bowl away and yawned. "No more. I think a bath, then bed for me. Did you get through Aaron okay?"

"I would have felt better if I'd had company."

"Aw, Mom." I ducked my head.

The Eye of the Storm

"I know, I'm sorry. I'm just so angry! The storm tore down the cannas just as I was about to finish my painting."

Disaster. It was a beautiful painting that she'd promised me for my room. I got up and hugged her, my ear brushing her chin; she's tall besides being gorgeous. "I'm sorry, too."

"Oh, pooh. I can finish it from memory. I just hate to have them destroyed."

That's Mom. Unpredictable, flighty, yes, but touched with an otherworld quality. Aaron had caused death and destruction everywhere, but only the cannas would stay in her memory.

Wallowing in the tub, I thought about her, and my father. Both of them were subject to quicksilver mood changes. Perhaps that's why they got along. It used to bother me a lot—their dedication to their career choices—but not any longer. I'd found my own way, made my own choice about my future.

I finally snuggled into bed, wearing a thin cotton nightshirt to protect me from the cool murmur of the air conditioner. I thought about that poor Stacy. It was, according to my digital radio clock, about a quarter to seven. She was to have been operated on at six. A subdural hematoma can be minor or major. Depending on which, she'd have to have some hair cut, and her scalp shaved. What an awful thing. Bright scarves could help. I fell asleep thinking that I'd look through my drawers tomorrow to find some scarves, and maybe, even, borrow some from Mom. I felt responsible for her.

When I woke up, there were birds chirping outside and I knew I'd slept more than twelve hours. I got up, put on white shorts and an I Love Texas T, and headed downstairs.

Dad was sitting at the breakfast table, his long nose almost into his coffee cup.

"Are you drinking that?" I asked cheerfully. "Or inhaling it?" I felt so good, so rested, I didn't notice his gloomy face until I'd poured myself a cup and sat down. "What's wrong? Did you lose a patient?" I'd seen that look before, and it had usually been because of a death in someone else's family. "Dad?"

He roused himself. "Oh, yes. I did lose a patient. Not the way you mean, though. She didn't die. That young woman, that Stacy you called her, she disappeared from recovery after the operation."

"She what?" I'd been in the process of lifting my cup to my mouth, but then I spilled the coffee all over my white shorts. Grabbing at the napkins in the holder, I soaked up some of the brown liquid, not moving, not breathing. Later, I found a few blisters on my legs, but I was sure I hadn't felt them. "How?"

"If I knew that," he snapped, "I'd know where to look for her." Then he said, "Sorry. I didn't mean that."

"I know." I crumpled up the wet napkins and threw them across toward the wastebasket. They missed. "What happened?"

"Dr. Jessup removed the clot. It was a small one, causing only minimal pressure on the brain. She was brought into recovery, he used the usual procedure to bring her out from under the anesthetic."

I nodded, knowing about that. I'd never been through it, but I could imagine a strange doctor's face looming over me, asking simple questions: two plus two, name, age, address, until the doctor is sure the pa-

The Eye of the Storm 45

tient hasn't had a relapse, or a bad reaction to the anesthetic. "What did she say?"

"Stacy Smith, age twenty-two. She passed all the other questions except her address. Dr. Jessup said she was cagey about that."

"Smith." I felt the heat of the cup penetrating my fingers. I set it down. "Then what happened?"

"Then there was a big ruckus in emergency. Guy came in with a snake bite. We didn't know what to do. Called Houston, and they said to get him on a 'copter immediately. But the guys, the pilots, had already left the hospital, thinking there wouldn't be any more emergencies. We had to locate one to uplift the patient to Houston. When we got back to recovery her bed was empty. The only other strange thing was a broken light bulb by the door to the parking lot, and a wheelchair was found outside."

"A wheelchair? Doesn't that look like someone transported her out of the hospital?"

"Oh, I don't know." Dad scratched his chin, where two days' growth itched. "We called the police, and they searched for her, but no luck."

"That's weird, wasn't she bandaged? Wouldn't she stick out like a sore thumb?"

Dad shrugged. "Not necessarily. We're not in the dark ages. A surgeon doesn't have to shave the whole head. The bandage only covered part of the left side of her head. A scarf could have covered it easily."

"Where would she get a scarf?" Dad didn't answer; I'd gotten him with that one. "And why was the wheelchair by the door?"

"The police figured she'd had a burst of strength after waking up in a strange place. It happens. They thought she'd probably used it herself, maybe to get to the phone by the door and call someone. Maybe she called that Todd."

"There was an area code. He couldn't have gotten to the hospital in such a short time."

"They checked the cab companies too. Nothing there. I'd like to know what happened. But it's not our problem now."

"What do you mean?"

"It's never the hospital's problem when a patient decides to leave. Unless, of course, it's a mental case. Someone who is a potential danger to society or him/herself."

"Never? What does that mean? This has happened before?"

Dad chortled. "In just about every hospital, I suspect, at one time or another. When I was interning in Michigan, we lost a guy with two broken legs. When I was a resident, there was an old man crippled up with arthritis. This geezer couldn't even walk, had to have a kidney removed, yet he was still drinking in the hospital. His bummy friends were sneaking booze in, but one night they didn't show. I guess, rather than drying out, he decided to get out." Dad laughed. "At least we knew how he did it. He tied sheets together and went out the window. The others, most of them, we never even knew how."

"What does the hospital do then? Put out a search warrant?"

"No. They do the same thing we did last night. Call the police, and if the patient isn't found in a few hours, it's forgotten."

"Forgotten?" My voice was small. "All those patients running around, needing medical attention, and they're forgotten?"

The Eye of the Storm 47

"Tessa." I was in for a lecture. Again. "First of all, a hospital cannot treat a patient who does not want to be treated. Secondly, we usually have enough problems with the ones who do want medical help. And thirdly, no hospital wants to admit losing a patient. It's bad publicity, especially for a small hospital like Lake Watson. The cops understand that; they won't give out the story to the news media."

I really didn't want to hear about fourthly.

"Fourthly," Dad announced, "the hospital is only responsible when the patient is in the hospital. If he or she leaves, the hospital is not liable. It's only on those silly TV shows that a doctor acts like a detective, finds the patient and drags him back for treatment."

I got it. Nobody was going to do a thing about Stacy. Dad went on with fifthly and sixthly, and frankly I was glad when he wound down and went upstairs to hit the hay.

Well, if he, they, no one was going to search for the missing Stacy, could I?

How? What could I do? I couldn't even remember that stupid telephone number. I sat as slumped as Dad had been when I'd come down all chipper. I leaned my elbows on the table and rubbed my temples, looking into my mind the way a gypsy looks into a crystal ball. Squinching my eyes shut, I concentrated and concentrated.

I'd have bet anything that it wouldn't work. It's a good thing I had no one to bet with, because it did. I couldn't believe it, but there it was, all wobbly and on a pink background too.

I didn't have time to wonder about the cells and stuff that make up the brain. I just hopped up to the wall phone and scribbled it down with one of Mom's zillion markers on a pad. Purple, that time. 555-9145. Of course! The area code began with four.

Now what? My wonderful brain responded with, "Why not let your fingers do the walking?" Good idea, I told it, knowing that if I'd told anyone else that I had conversations with my brain they might label me bonkers.

I got more coffee, and the phone book from the cabinet. When I was settled at the table with everything, including the scratch pad and pen, I found myself in a maze of area codes.

Who had ever thought up where to put area codes? Someone crazier than me, that's for sure. Probably a committee of loonies from the phone company, throwing darts at maps of the United States and Canada. How else could anyone explain New York, Alabama, and Fresno, California, all beginning with the first digit of two. And the fours! They were so widespread they made as much sense as a connect-the-dot game without any numbers.

I made a list of the fours, putting the names of the areas beside them and found there were twelve. If my luck persisted, Todd, whoever he was, would end up to be the last on the list. Could a person plead temporary insanity for a phone bill?

Shutting my eyes, I whirled my index finger above the list, and poked it. San Jose, California. The wall phone seemed so far away, but I willed myself to it. I punched out the number, my whole being shaking.

"Hello," came the quivery voice across the miles.

A little old lady, I thought. "Hi," I said brightly. "Could I speak to Todd, please?"

"Who?"

"Todd?"

The Eye of the Storm   49

A few more who's and a final yell of "Todd!" and she said, "I don't think there's anyone here by that name. There was a person named Ted, I think. But he flew away yesterday and hasn't come back."

Terrific.

My fingers walked and punched numbers from Alberta, Canada, through Montana, to Pittsburgh, Pennsylvania. I glanced at the digital clock on the stove and was alarmed to see that it was 7:53. That left seven minutes until daytime rates when I would have to stop my game of area-code roulette. My insanity did not include wasting money.

The next call was to San Francisco. Bingo! "Hi, may I speak to Todd, please?"

The voice was low pitched, and a little groggy. "This is he."

I'd forgotten the time difference would make it 6:00 a.m. there, and his answer made me very nervous. Heart pinging, I plunged ahead. "I hope I didn't wake you, but do you, ah, do you know a, a, Stacy?"

"Stacy?" The voice came alive. It was loud, still husky, but loud. "Who is this?"

"I," I began nervously, "I, er, work in a hospital here in Texas, and this young woman came in last night, well really the night before, during a hurricane, and she had a head injury and she gave me this number to call and ask for Todd, and so I did what she asked me, but now she's sort of disappeared, and I thought you could tell me, I mean..."

"Is this some sort of joke?" Todd's voice cut through my rambling. "Stacy, as I'm sure you know, is in a sanitorium. Why can't you ghouls leave things alone?"

"Ghouls?" I questioned in a whisper. As his tone had gotten louder, mine had retreated to the back of my throat. "Is, ah, is the sanitorium in Texas?"

"Of course, and you know that! You're a kid, I can tell from your voice! What happened? You find an old newspaper clipping?"

"No. No, really, please, listen, she was in the hospital, and then she went into a coma, and then she got operated on for a subdural hematoma, and after that she disappeared, but before all that, she gave me your number and seemed scared."

"Oh, sure." Todd answered my lousy delivery with sarcasm. "When she was in a coma, she still managed to give you my phone number. Tell me the truth. Who put you up to this? The *National Enquirer*?"

"No, you see, it was before the coma, and she was really upset, then she got injured again, somehow, but after the operation, when she came out from under the anesthetic, she said her name was Stacy Smith."

"Smith!" He actually chuckled. "You know the real name is Harlon, now you hear me, and hear me good. I'm sick and tired of you newspaper hounds, but of all the dirty tricks that have been played on me, this is the worst. If I ever find out who put you up to this, I'll sue for twenty million dollars. Don't think I won't!"

Bam! He hung up. *Twenty million dollars?* Could a person be sued for that much over a phone call? And there I was worried about a little thing like the bill for the calls. Maybe I should have found out the name of the sanitorium. I could voluntarily commit myself.

Automatically, I checked the clock. Eight on the nose. I heard my mother's high-heeled slippers on the stairs. I hid the evidence of my phone ramble, and by

The Eye of the Storm 51

the time she appeared at the kitchen door I was seated innocently at the table.

"Morning darlin'." She swished by me to the coffee. "Want some cinnamon rolls?"

"Sure," I answered brightly. That should have given her a clue that I was up to something. I detest breakfast. I like to eat most any other time, but I never seem to be hungry after a night's sleep. The robot who replaces my mother in the morning did not notice, however.

She did by her second cup of coffee, though. "Hmmm, I'm glad to see you eating this morning. You'll need your energy; we have to take the tape off the windows."

"Oh, groan."

Actually, it wasn't all that bad. Mom had gotten a clothes steamer for Christmas and we hauled it out. Worked like a charm, and I was sweet as rhubarb pie; yes, I did think occasionally about Max, but mostly my mind went over and over the conversation with Todd. I had the guilts about the phone calls, too. I tried to think of ways to pay for them, and I tried not to think of having to explain it. I get a good allowance, but a lot of it goes for gas for the bug. I wondered if I could borrow the clothes steamer, go around the neighborhood and charge for removing other people's tape.

Then, of course, I wondered what else to do about the missing Stacy.

Taking the sticky mess of tape to the garbage pail, I saw the morning newspaper, rolled up and sticking out of a bush. Our newspaper girl is a snot-nosed twelve-year-old who will never make it as a ball player. I dug it out and started back into the house. *Newspapers?* "See you later, Mom," I said. "I'm going to the library."

Chapter Five

"Harlon. I guess the spelling is H-a-r-l-o-n. The first name is Stacy." I stood in front of the massive mahogany desk that seemed to dwarf Lake Watson's small library. I'd been there before and gotten to know the librarian, Mrs. Terry, really well, looking up microsurgery and other medical things that Dad's library didn't cover.

She was youngish, blond, enthusiastic and helpful. "I guess this isn't one of your medical problems."

"No. I got interested by hearing about a scandal recently, and thought I'd check it out." Librarians don't care why, only that you're interested.

I was wrong. She did care. "Surely you haven't given up the idea of being a doctor?"

"Pardon me?" That was very hard to say when I wanted to yell, "What?" The *idea*!

The Eye of the Storm   53

Mrs. Terry poked a pencil over her left ear and smiled. "The Harlon case. It's such a story. And you know, they've done so many of those fact-crime books lately—Ted Bundy, the Von Bulow case—I've even dallied with writing about it myself. Attempted murder, insanity, money, it has all the qualities of a miniseries."

I felt weak-kneed. "Yes, you're so right. And frankly, between us, I am thinking about writing now. I'd just love to see the facts."

Mrs. Terry beamed at me with the assurance of one who knows that sixteen-year-olds change their minds all the time. One day a doctor, the next a writer, and perhaps a firewoman in the fall. "It seems like a fascinating story," I added, wondering what the story was.

"It is." Mrs. Terry rose and, still beaming, looked down at me from the other side of the desk. "The whole newspaper coverage is on microfilm, but I saved all the original clippings from then, plus I've got printouts from the time of Stacy's birth. You, uh, you're not thinking about a book or anything, are you?"

"Oh, no," I assured her. "I was thinking about an article next fall for the school newspaper."

She frowned. "It's hardly the subject matter for that." Then, magically, her face cleared. "Oh, I see. Because Stacy was a teenager at the time. How clever!"

I didn't feel clever, but I felt lucky, lucky, lucky. In no time at all, I was sitting at a table with the yellowed news clippings in front of me. I couldn't wait to find out what had happened, and although I'm not a speed reader, I became so caught up in them that I almost became one.

The coverage began when Stacy Jennings Harlon was born in the old hospital in Clute, Texas. Then picked up on her several years later when her socialite parents were drowned in a boating accident. Her grandfather, Sherman Jennings, took the young orphan in, and she lived in his mansion on the outskirts of Lake Watson. Several years later, the grandfather died, making Stacy an heiress. Sherman had been the father of her mother, and his only other child, David, had moved back into the mansion to take care of Stacy.

David Jennings, who shared equally in the millions that Sherman had left, was also the executor of his father's estate. Stacy's share would not be turned over to her properly until her eighteenth birthday. The money had come from oil, where else? Texas being Texas and all that.

Stacy got into so much trouble as a teenager, her uncle called her as "madcap" as Zelda Fitzgerald was in the twenties. Several antics were described in detail. At fifteen, she'd been kicked out of Hindell's Academy For Young Ladies for getting drunk, smoking in bed and causing a fire. When her uncle decided to have her tutored at home, she tried to push her tutor into the swimming pool.

Then she eloped with a truck driver who dumped her in New Mexico and who called David Jennings with a demand for money in return for telling him where Stacy was. The truck driver was arrested for taking a minor across the state line, and a sullen Stacy was returned to her Uncle David who refused comment to the press. She was sixteen then, and the next article dealt with her seventeenth birthday party when she stripped to the buff on top of the high diving board above the swimming pool. The press speculated that the hired caterer had called the police out of resentment; his food had ended up in a food fight. Anyway, there were quantities of drugs found on the premises.

The Eye of the Storm 55

There were a few more incidents listed. An attempted suicide. Stacy arrested for drunk driving. Another food fight in a restaurant. I was getting a picture of a terribly troubled child/woman. No wonder Mrs. Terry had understood. Lord, there have been times when I've wanted to act up like that.

David Jennings then sent her to a shrink. There was nothing for a few months, and then an article by Stacy herself, in which she said, *I was mixed up about myself and all that money.* It went on to say that she'd come to terms with herself and the money, and was now devoting her time as a volunteer at a child abuse center. I had to wonder about that. Had she been abused? One reporter asked that, but her answer was evasive.

The next mention of Stacy was when she announced her engagement to Todd Lewis. *Todd!* They had met at the center, and although Todd was six years older than she, and the son of an offshore driller, they'd fallen immediately in love. The papers seemed to be all for the romantic couple, although one referred to him as "Cinderfella. The young, poor but talented architect who's snared one of Texas's richest women."

"Ha!" I said. At seventeen she was a woman to the press?

Finally, I got to "The Crime." There were the headlines: Stacy Jennings Harlon Accused of Knifing Uncle. "Wow," I muttered. I scanned the article, then read it completely. It said that Stacy's uncle, David Jennings, had demanded that Stacy break her engagement to Todd. They were still living in the old Jennings mansion, and one night after a terrible argument in the study, Stacy allegedly went into the kitchen, took a large chef's knife, returned to the study and stabbed her uncle. Then she went up to her room and went to sleep. I thought that was weird.

The police found her there, her white cotton nightgown smeared with her uncle's blood. David Jennings survived the attack, and his statement, plus the blood on the nightgown, was enough to make the charge stick. The newspapers had a field day, concentrating on Stacy's earlier wild ways, and ignoring her later activities as a volunteer.

There was also a map of old man Jennings's vast estate in Lake Watson and a detailed drawing of the interior of the house. A clichéd X marked the spot of the attack in the study.

It sounded to me like she was damned before the trial, and the trial itself was so brief it took only a day and a half to judge her innocent by reason of insanity. She was then sentenced to an indefinite stay in Lake Watson's most prestigious sanitorium, Sylvan Glade.

Another clipping answered my next question: Who would get all the millions? Uncle David, of course, quoted by one reporter as saying, "All I want to do is live quietly now that my poor, darling Stacy is finally being taken care of. I pray she gets well and comes back to me, but if her confinement to Sylvan Glade is permanent, then I will take it as God's will."

"Uh-huh." Stacy gets locked up for life at seventeen, and dear uncle gets all the money.

Another reporter, from a sleazier paper, described David Jennings's actions in court, and sounded as if he were on Stacy's side. Uncle David had taken off his shirt in court to show the wound! And that was the only newspaper that reported Stacy as repeating over and over again, "I didn't do it."

The Eye of the Storm 57

A few more clippings told me that Todd Lewis was outside the jail when Stacy was moved to Sylvan Glade, but was not allowed to speak to or touch her. The news media surrounded him, asking about his future plans. At first he answered, "To leave this stinking town, and get as far away from Texas as possible."

As the crowd surged closer, he knocked the camera out of one reporter's hand and punched another. Those pictures were blurred, yet one photo captured a strained-into-agony face. So that was Todd. Now I understood his attitude on the phone, and why he wouldn't, or couldn't, believe me.

The final clipping read: Update of Jennings-Harlon Case. "It has now been a year since the heiress, Stacy Jennings Harlon, was admitted to Sylvan Glade for the attempted murder of her uncle, David Jennings."

There was a recap on all involved. David Jennings was living alone in the mansion, traveling occasionally. Todd Lewis lived in San Francisco and was a promising young architect. He had no comment for the reporter. Well, who could blame him?

And as for Stacy? The head of Sylvan Glade, a Dr. Jocelyn Boden, told the reporter that Stacy had gone into a severe decline and might never be released. The article went on to describe Sylvan Glade as an elegant old mansion with swimming pools, gardens, elegantly appointed rooms and an atmosphere of luxury.

Still, I felt an overwhelming sadness. Stacy had been only a year older than I was now when she'd been shut up in her gilded prison, possibly forever. She'd started out badly, sure, but then had chosen to work with abused kids. Could she be so awful that she knifed her uncle?

The more important question though: Was she my Stacy? Studying all the yellowed black-and-white photos didn't tell me. A posed studio shot of Stacy showed a glamorous type with long, light hair. Her eyes had been made up with a heavy hand, and her false eyelashes looked like caterpillars. Her lips were pouty as though she was trying to tell the world that she was a wild and wicked woman. She'd been fifteen when it was taken.

In contrast, the shot of her outside the jail, in bright sunlight, showed a defeated attitude with one hand raised covering half her face. The others were mostly of David Jennings who appeared to be a tall man with slight pouches under his eyes. It had been five years; could those pouches have become bags? Or was I imagining a resemblance to the man on the stairs?

Mrs. Terry crept over to my table on crepe-soled shoes. "Isn't it exciting?"

I thrust my head up so fast it almost rolled off the back of my neck. "Yes!" I said too loudly. "I mean, yes it is," I added when I saw her index finger automatically seek her pursed lips.

"It's almost three o'clock, dear. The library closes early on Friday—summer hours. You can always come back." She efficiently scooped up the clippings and returned them to her file folder. There was no doubt as to whose property they were, and I wondered if she'd had regrets letting me see them.

"I'm so grateful," I said, standing. Her eyes evaded mine and I thought I might have hit the old nail on the head. "I really think you should write about this. It would make a wonderful fact-crime book, but, frankly, the reason I'm so interested is not only for the school paper. It's a little more complicated than that, and all I

can say for now is that the ending might change soon."
There, now I had her attention. Curiosity abounded in her gaze. "You know my father is a doctor?" She nodded; everyone in Lake Watson knew about the new doc in town. "Well, then, you see, don't you?"

"Of course," she answered, and of course she didn't see, but didn't want to look stupid, either. "If there's anything I can do to help..."

"There is." I lowered my voice to just above a whisper. "We need copies of these clippings, and of course we'll pay for them, but no one should know about this except us. Can I trust you?"

She fell for it. Hook, line, and I was the stinker. Perhaps I wouldn't want to be a firewoman in the fall; I might make a better con woman.

"Oh, I won't breathe a word, and I can get copies on Monday from my husband's office machine."

"Great." I was afraid of asking her if she could trust her husband. I didn't want to push my luck.

She walked me to the door, clutching the folder as if it were pure gold. When I'd come into the small library, she'd been having an average day, but now her step was springy and her smile edged with excitement.

I smiled back and went quickly down the front steps, afraid that a fit of insane laughter might burst out from me.

Chapter Six

It wasn't so funny by the time I got into the bug. I'd been clever and smart, but still I'd pulled a con game. I can get away with things like that sometimes, like the time I'd talked Dad into selling Girl Scout cookies to his patients. When I'd gotten first prize for the amount sold, he sat me down and told me, in no uncertain words, how dishonest I'd been. I felt dishonest about Mrs. Terry, but I needed those copies. I cheered myself up by thinking that maybe I'd be right in the end. Then Mrs. Terry would really have something to write about.

The bug turned left, almost on its own, and I was on the right road for the hospital. Well, why not? I was sure the hospital was still in chaos and needed help. I needed to help. After all, I didn't know how to proceed, and maybe, just maybe, if I did help I wouldn't feel so guilty about running up phone bills and conning librarians.

The Eye of the Storm 61

My days at Lake Watson Community General are never enough for me anyway. Tuesday, Thursday and Saturday, from twelve to five. Aaron had been on Wednesday, and today was Friday. I'd have to get Mrs. Nettles to approve my working the third day in a row.

I was almost to her office when I heard, "Tessa! Tessa." Turning, I saw Max bearing down on me. He looked like he'd been through another hurricane. The black hair tumbled into his face and his eyes were blue and bloodshot.

"Hi?" It came out like a question because I didn't believe he was there. It wasn't his day either; his were Sunday, Tuesday and Thursday. Tuesday had been the only time, before Aaron, that I'd had to put up with his arrogance. "What are you doing here?"

"I couldn't stay away. What about you?"

I had to smile back. "No, neither could I. Is there anything to do?"

"Lots," he said. "The other TeeVees aren't, well, you know."

I knew, but it wasn't the sort of thing one discussed openly. A lot of them had joined up in a spurt of community service, then hadn't liked getting the dirty work we got. I mean, go scrub vomit off the floor! "Maybe," I offered, "they had things to do at home." Like going to the beach, I didn't add. "Is Mrs. Nettles around?"

"She's upstairs, doing some of the TeeVee work. I think she feels badly that the troops haven't shown up."

"We're the only ones?"

"No, no. Maria is up in pediatrics, Sally in ICU and Vern is on the med floor. Most of the beds are full, though, and you know?"

Max stood in front of me. Looking up, I saw how tired he was. "Have you been here all night again?" I asked softly.

He hesitated, his smile slipping, then admitted, "After the diner closed at two, I went home, showered, took a nap, then I couldn't sleep anymore and came back. Look, I have to talk to you about something. I have to—could we have coffee?"

"Sure," I said uncertainly.

When we were seated at the same booth Dad and I had sat at Thursday morning, I examined his face again. There was a telltale blue shadow under his nose and on his chin. "I guess you could have shaved, too," I said, trying to not feel uncomfortable. I hadn't realized how skinny the table was, and had to turn my knees away. They were almost touching his.

I'd embarrassed him. He ran his hand over the stubble. "I forgot. I'm not used to it yet."

Oh no, I thought. I hadn't meant to do that. There are boys who don't have to shave until they're twenty, and others who have mustaches at thirteen, but I'd never commented on either before. "I didn't mean anything, it was only an observation." I could feel a blush hitting my cheeks. I hoped it wouldn't creep all over my face.

The waitress came and asked what we wanted. Feeling worse, I ordered a cheeseburger and a Coke. After Max ordered coffee, I said, "I'm sorry. I skipped lunch and I'll pay for mine."

"No, you won't." He played with the salt and pepper shakers, moving one in front of the other and reversing them. "I invited you. The cheeseburgers aren't real good here, though. We have better ones at the diner. We don't order preformed patties. Ours are sloppy but real."

"Oh." I relied on my usual snappy response. Envying his possession of the shakers, I wished I had them to play with. "I'd like to try them sometime."

"How about tomorrow night after a movie?"

It came so fast, I didn't know what to say. Having a mental picture of all the hearts I'd heard Max had broken didn't help. "Why?" slipped out before I knew it. "I mean, why are you asking me out, Max? All we do is fight." The rest followed as quickly as the first.

He made a noise and leaned back into the red booth. "You really are honest, aren't you? I guess that's one of the reasons I like you."

"Huh?" He liked me? Because I was honest? I wasn't feeling honest, not after the day I'd put in stealing phone time and conning a librarian.

Max was still leaning back. "What if I told you that all the rumors you've heard about me aren't true? What if I told you that I'm not the chauvinist everyone, including you, thinks? What if—oh, never mind."

The waitress was plunking down our orders then, and Max clammed up as if afraid she would overhear him. The cheeseburger was lukewarm and I knew he was right about the preformed pattie. What else was he right about? I picked up my pickle and waved it at him. "Max, you're trying to tell me what? So, get on with it." Yep, I was impatient, and that covered up a lot of anxiety on my part. I had just taken a bite of the cheeseburger when he answered.

"I want to be a nurse."

"What?" I swear I didn't mean for that bite of meat and cheese to cross the table and hit his shirtfront.

"See?" He started to get up, but was clumsy about it. The booth seemed to wedge him in.

"Sit down!" I ordered, grabbing a napkin. He did, and reaching across the table I sponged off his shirt. "You're right. I certainly could use a cheeseburger that's old-fashioned and hand patted."

He laughed a sort of choking laugh. It wasn't his greatest.

I met his eyes. "Hey, I think that's great. You'll be a good one, and you know how important nurses are. Dad always says they're the lifeline between the patients and the doctors."

He was playing with the shakers again. "Then why don't you want to be one too?"

I had to think it over. It took a few awkward moments, then I said thoughtfully, "I'm not sure. Part of it has to do with my father, part of it has to do with stereotypes which irritate me—I mean, I can become a doctor with ease now, whereas before it would have been more difficult for me as a female. Prestige has something to do with it, but mostly it's a passion to heal, and I think my passion will involve children, and I can't give you any more reasons now. I just want to be a doctor." We were both silent; he was watching my flushed face. "Tell me why you want to be a nurse," I finally said.

He hesitated, too. I could see how difficult it was for him to talk about. Then he sighed as if giving in to the need to talk. "I told you about all the kids in my family, didn't I? There are too many of us to afford much education. There's a three-year nursing school in Houston, and if I get in there I can still work for my uncle—my father died a few years ago..." His sentence trailed off; so did his eyes.

"I'm so sorry," I said, wanting to touch his hand, wanting to communicate my sympathy. I didn't. Not the right time or place.

He picked up again. "Leukemia. I helped to nurse him while my mother took care of the kids. Anyway, at that time I thought about being a doctor, but the realities hit me, and I figured it all out. Just a few years after graduating from high school I can be a licensed R.N. Then I can think about going on for my B.Sc., my masters, or whatever. And I might want to become a doctor then. In the meantime, I like being that 'lifeline' you mentioned. The patients need it; maybe I need to be it."

I took the shaker away from him to salt my hamburger. Our fingers brushed against each other's. He handed me the pepper and I smiled. "I understand. And that sort of answers your question about me. I think I have to admit that I'm more interested in diagnosing and healing than in nursing the patient. Does that make me a bad person?"

"The worst!" he said almost deadpan. "I've never met such a horrible person."

"Ho, ho, I see a twinkle in those bloodshot eyes. Get stuffed!" We laughed together, then I added, "Did you say something about a movie tomorrow night and a sloppy hamburger?"

"The sloppiest."

We left the coffee shop side by side. It felt good. I knew his deep dark secret now, and I could understand why he'd pulled so much macho business. I bet myself that I was one of the few who knew.

Mrs. Nettles was back in her office and waved at me to come in. I said to Max, "What time tomorrow, and want to take my car?"

"That ugly old thing?" He grinned. "I'll be over about seven, okay?"

I stopped him from walking away. "Hey! Don't you want my address?"

"Nope, I know where you live. I've been by the house dozens of times—don't you *ever* do any gardening? Besides, I live about three streets over on Cedar Grove."

My mouth was still open in astonishment as he waved and stepped into an elevator.

Chapter Seven

Being assigned as a "floater" is not usually my favorite thing, but that's what I got on Saturday. Floaters do general duty for all the floor nurses' stations, which means taking specimens down to the lab, picking up medicine from the pharmacy, helping patients prepare to leave and wheeling them downstairs, along with a lot of other running around collecting and delivering packages, messages, or whatever.

The only floor that TeeVees are not allowed on is five, the psycho ward. That afternoon, I left the pharmacy with Rudy, the aide, both of us wheeling carts of medication, and when we got on the back elevator, he pushed five. Something clicked in my mind. Of course, I had to get into Sylvan Glade and see for myself if Stacy Jennings Harlon was there! I could relax if she was. If she wasn't, well, I'd face that problem when I had to.

"Is Dr. Waite in his office today?" I asked Rudy.

"Chure," he said. "Saturday he always there."

"Thanks." I got off on med, delivered my tray and asked the head nurse if I could take my break. I could, and I went down to the cafeteria.

Barging in on Dr. Oliver Waite, the hospital psychiatrist, in his office would not be the proper thing for a TeeVee to do, but I hoped to catch him on a break. I'd met him at the welcoming party for our family, and at several other parties since then. Lake Watson's medical community goes for parties, family picnics, and socializing at the country club.

The cafeteria would be a perfect place to talk to Dr. Waite. In a small nonteaching hospital like Lake Watson, most of the staff love to talk to us TeeVees if we have specific questions, or show an interest in a particular career.

The cafeteria is a small one, since it is only for staff. Its walls are blinding white, and its features are chrome. The coffee shop upstairs may be tacky, but it's cozy compared to the ambience of chrome and fluorescent lights that make people and food a little green around the edges. And no Dr. Waite.

For fifteen minutes I sat and watched the door, nibbling on a grilled cheese whose bread looked moldy. During the last five minutes of my break, Jordan strode in, looking like an ad from *Modern Physician*. I swear his whites were whiter than the walls, and his stethoscope twinkled with reflected light. He saw me, got a cranberry juice and took a chair at my table, all in his own graceful style. "I'm sorry about the other night," he said promptly. "I hope there aren't any hard feelings."

Instinct told me to be quiet. I watched him.

"I didn't mean to imply that you weren't trying to help." *Trying?* I bit my tongue. He lifted his glass to me. "I was fatigued. I don't really think of you as a child at all. I shouldn't have treated you that way. As a matter of fact, why don't we have dinner tonight?"

Dinner? With Jordan? I'd once loved the daydream of such an event. Candlelight, wine, holding hands across the table. I tried to imagine him eating a sloppy hamburger. No way, and poof! The daydream went bye-bye.

"What about it?" Jordan asked with a winning smile, yet adding a touch of anxiety as though I would devastate him if I turned him down. Uh-uh, I saw something else, most likely fear. Proctorships are hard to come by; grades and recommendations have to be high, then there is at least a year of correspondence between all concerned.

I didn't answer. I was still intrigued by what would happen if I didn't. Of course Jordan couldn't know that Dad would judge him strictly on his own merit, not by what I said. My whining about what a pompous donkey's behind Jordan was wouldn't make a bit of difference.

"We could go to that new Tex-Mex place on Watson Road." He was pleading now.

He was pulling all the tricks, too. I love Tex-Mex food, as he knew, having spent time eating Mom's tacos supreme. Cute.

I glanced at my watch quickly, knowing I had about one minute to turn the tables on him. Con woman away! "Gee, I'd love to Jordan, but I have a date tonight."

He looked properly crushed, but couldn't hide another feeling. I think it was relief. I pushed away my nibbled sandwich and said, "But you could do me another favor, if you would." I got up to leave; he had a wide-eyed expression. "Would you call Dr. Waite and ask him if I could tour the psyche ward? I'm thinking about becoming a psychiatrist, and I'd adore to see it. With your clout, I'd be in good standing with him, don't you think?"

Gentleman to the core, he rose too, and agreed right away. "Of course! Then we'll be friends again?"

"Oh, Jordan." I sighed, touching his arm lightly as though regretting my turndown. "We've always been friends. I'm a floater today, but if you leave a message for me on med, I'll get it. And any other time you want to have dinner, let me know. I must dash now." Too, too, but it worked.

"I'd be delighted."

I dashed away, thinking about the time I'd wasted daydreaming of him, when I could have been with Max. I never said I was the smartest person in the world.

Back on med, I was grinning to myself. Nope, I wasn't the smartest, but neither was Jordan. He did come through, though. Later that afternoon, sure enough, the message was at the desk! It was short, to the point, and sweet to me: Your appointment is at five. Best, J.

By 4:30 I was antsy; 4:59 made me remember Stacy, and Todd's phone number. At that point I was on the stairs with my tongue practically hanging out of my mouth. What would I say to him? To Dr. Waite?

Oh my gosh, I should have realized that there would be a gate onto five. There was a bell; I rang it, not wanting to be late. "Hi, I'm Tessa Murphy and I have an appointment with..."

The Eye of the Storm 71

"I know." The nurse who'd come to the gate was large. Did she have to be? I mean, to deal with the patients? She let me in, saying, "You should have taken the elevator. It's much easier."

"Uh-huh, sure, yeah, you're right."

Dr. Waite's office was to the left and behind a small nurses' station tucked between two more grille gates. I hoped my hand wasn't sweating as the doc shook it. "Tessa, how nice to see you again." He smiled that half smile that I now recalled. I'd always felt he could see into my inner self. Maybe everyone feels like that in the presence of a shrink. Like he could stamp my forehead with a diagnosis of normal or abnormal. "I don't think you've grown and I know how much you young people hate that phrase anyway, but I do think you have matured. After Jordan asked me to see you, I checked your record. Although you've been here a short time, you've shown yourself to be quite apt. Do sit down."

I did. "Tell me about yourself," he said.

Scratch my short career as a con woman. He seemed so interested that although I was weaving a myth, I tripped myself up more than once.

"I see, I see." He leaned back in his chair, putting both hands on a flat stomach. He was lean and hard. No fat on him. His hair was brown with flecks of gold appearing from the sun outside the window, and his eyes weren't distinctive in color. They were in energy. "Yes, I think I understand. I do some counseling for career changes in my private practice. You seem confused about everything but what you ultimately want to do. I remember feeling that kind of confusion. I started out thinking I wanted the fast buck as a dermatologist. Then I wondered about pathology. You can't believe it, I'm sure, but once I discovered psychiatry, I felt I'd found my niche. Now, your love for children might lead you toward OB/GYN, PD, or you might consider dealing with the autistic..."

He went on and on and, truthfully, I was fascinated.

"This has been so enjoyable," he said after a time, "that I hesitate to ask what you think."

"I've found it, er, enjoyable too," I said. I had to poke and prod myself to bring back the real reason for my being there. Then I wanted to dump the whole thing into Dr. Waite's lap. I couldn't, though; how would he take it? "I guess there aren't any easy answers, are there?"

"Never," he said firmly. "Now, would you like to see the wings? Most of my patients here are short-termers—clinically depressed, borderline schizophrenia, nervous breakdowns, that sort of thing. My more serious cases are at the state sanitorium."

We had walked outside the office by then. "How many patients do you have here?"

"We're full up. Twenty beds in each wing." Dr. Waite stopped. "Which one would you like to see, the loonies or the junkies?"

I was amazed, and showed it.

"Have to have a sense of humor to deal with what psychiatry involves. In group, patients have to feel comfortable; they tell each other they're crazy or junkies instead of mentally ill or drug abusers. Drunks too; we have four on the floor now." Dr. Waite hesitated. "You can come back to visit another time, but I only have time to show you one wing. I think I'd like you to see the junkies and drunks."

Whew. I didn't want to see them, but I was in his hands. Two of the drunks were being detoxified, and it was horrible. One of the kids was younger than me. I

The Eye of the Storm

hated to watch him rolling around and screaming for a drink. The junkies were pretty well off the stuff. Still, a couple of them weren't pretty to look at.

Back out in the hall, Dr. Waite saw my face. "You okay?" I nodded weakly. "All right, I'll tell you why I wanted to show you that. I'm thinking about setting up a program for the schools, perhaps a film, showing exactly what drugs and alcohol do to the system. When Jordan called me about you, I got the idea of asking you to help me with it. If someone doesn't stop kids from abusing substances, we are going to become a nation of junkies and alcoholics."

I gulped. What a can of worms I had opened. "I, er, I would like to think about that. Perhaps..."

"Take your time." Dr. Waite walked me to the elevator.

Whoa! I hadn't got what I'd come to get. "Er, Dr. Waite, I've heard a lot about Sylvan Glade and how fabulous it is. Do you think patients are helped more in such a posh atmosphere?"

"It's difficult to say," Dr. Waite mused. "Some patients don't know where they are, so of course it wouldn't matter. However, I do think color is important."

"Are you affiliated with Sylvan Glade?"

"I'm called in to consult once in a while." Dr. Waite pushed the elevator button. "But with only fifty beds, Dr. Boden and her staff take care of most problems. I believe she has two psychologists, besides the nurses, therapists and aides. It's a marvelous place—every time I go, I sneak a swim in the pool. It's an expensive place to be in, but you should see it."

"I'd love to!" I enthused so much I almost knocked him down. "Do you think it's possible?"

"Anything's possible." He stuffed his hands into his pockets. "However, you must understand that even if you go into psychiatry, jobs at places like that are few and far between."

"Oh, I know that. I'm curious about it, though. And I think I might be interested in your program, you know. It sounds like it's important."

That was all I needed to say; I could have asked him to call the president and he would have done it. I stood in that hall, waiting for him to come back from making the call to Dr. Boden, feeling like such a liar. Would it all be worth it? Do private eyes on television go through such trauma? No, of course not.

Small compensation. I don't know what Dr. Waite told Dr. Boden, but it probably had something to do with encouraging our young folk to follow in our footsteps. Anyway, he was back in minutes saying, "Tomorrow afternoon at 1:45. Visiting hours are at two, and she figures the patients wouldn't be upset seeing a stranger. She did suggest, though, that you try to look official, and wear your smock and name tag."

Wow. "Oh yes, I will. And thank you, Dr. Waite, thank you!"

"I'll appreciate your telling me what you think about Sylvan Glade. And we'll have to meet sometime next week about the program."

"Yeah, sure."

I had gone off duty at five anyway, but snuck out the back door for two reasons. One was so I wouldn't have to turn in my smock to Mrs. Nettles, who always seemed to be around. The second reason was that I wanted to see the exit where Stacy had exited. I checked the door carefully. It was too heavy for a sick person to push, especially one in a wheelchair. Although it was a bright, sunny June day in Texas, I tried to imagine what it had been like at night. She'd left the recovery room about 9:15, meaning that dark would have clothed the whole area except where the light was. It had been broken. Now, it had been replaced.

I checked my watch. "Yipes." It was after six and Max would be by at seven. My mother still didn't know I had a date. Had I intentionally forgotten to tell her? Maybe. I hadn't had a date in Texas yet. When I'd left Michigan, I'd left with my heart broken. I had been going with a boy for about a year, and right before the news about us moving came his news about wanting to play the field. Knowing Dennis, it was more like his wanting to play around, which I wasn't ready for.

I'd confided that in Tim, and Mom had guessed because that's one of the obvious reasons why a boy breaks up with a girl. It hadn't occurred to me until that second that I might have the same problem with Max. First-date jitters. Would they ever go away?

Hurrying home in the bug, I thought about what to wear. A skirt would be nice, since he'd only seen me at school in jeans or the hospital in whites.

After I pulled into the driveway, I realized I still had my smock on, and got an old ditty bag out of the trunk to stow it in. I didn't want any questions.

My parents were both sitting on the patio, Dad in a suit and Mom in a silk dress. "What's up?" I asked.

"We thought we'd go to the club for dinner," Dad answered, lifting his gin and tonic. "How long will it take you to get ready?"

"I have a date," I said slowly.

Silence. Mom broke it. "With whom?"

"Max Mitchell. I have to get ready. He'll be here at seven."

"Max Mitchell?" Both eyebrows arched above her eyes with surprise. "Isn't that the boy you hate?"

"I don't hate him anymore. I really don't. You'll like him, honestly."

Dad grinned at me, then Mom. "I already do like him. He's a fine boy and he'll be a fine nurse."

"A nurse!" Mom spluttered into her drink.

"How did you know?" I was stunned.

"I have my ways." Dad winked. "I've noticed him around the hospital. He's got a better way of dealing with patients than most of you TeeVees, including you, teacup."

I made a nasty face. "I'd better get changed. Have a nice dinner."

"You'll see us before we leave." My mother nestled firmly into the cushion of the wicker chair. "We'll have another drink before leaving. Your father may approve, but I have to see for myself."

As I was zooming up the stairs, I heard her say, "A nurse? Is the boy normal?"

Parents. Dad's approval had made me uncomfortable, and Mom's attitude had made me feel worse. If I'd brought home a punker with pink hair and tights, she'd say it was a phase, and Dad would kick him out of the house.

A shower knocked some of the jitters out of me, and my hair frizzed out in clouds. Good. It was fashionable, and Max had probably never seen me with it out of braids or tails. I piled on some makeup and wiped off half of it. I wanted to look natural. Stacy's photo came back to haunt me. Tomorrow, maybe, I'd find the answer.

The Eye of the Storm 77

My closet laughed at me. It was chock full of jeans, white ducks and other pants, but then I discovered a tropical outfit Mom had bought me last March. A long skirt splashed with flowers, a yellow halter and a jacket that had shoulder pads! It might be too dressy for a movie and sloppy hamburgers, but I put it on anyway. A white sling bag and white sandals and I was ready, I hoped.

A glimpse in the hall mirror told me I looked good. Oh, I'd never be devastating like Mom, but no one would gag on viewing me, either.

I almost lost my newfound poise when I got downstairs. Max was sitting on a wicker chair talking to Mom. Dad was at the bar by the dining room, fixing more drinks. He whistled at me, and asked if I wanted a soda. When he said that Max was having one, I joined the crowd. Mom sparkled at me. "Sweetie, Tessa, you look great!" She must have made up her mind that Max was normal because she then sparkled at him. "Doesn't she look wonderful?"

Max turned. I saw his face. He agreed. I was embarrassed.

They offered us dinner at the club, but we turned it down. When I started to get into the driver's seat of the bug, I thought about Max's not having a car. Honestly, it wasn't a case of female pleasing male that made me say, "Would you like to drive?"

"Could I?" He leaped at the chance like a kid at roller skates. When we were on the road he said, "Hey, this car may look ugly, but it acts like a star."

"It's my brother Tim's. He rebuilt it." First-date jitters went bye-bye. Max had to know all about Tim, and then I heard all about Phil, Karen, Christie, Alicia, Bernie and the baby of the family, Bitsy. I guess it doesn't sound like a fantastic conversation to say we talked about our families, but the way he told stories about those kids made me want to meet them. And I'd never met anyone who could stand for me to talk about Tim for more than five seconds. Any boy, I mean. I'd had some girl friends back in Michigan who were fascinated by my big brother, but since being in Texas, I hadn't made any fast friends. Funny, I told Max about that. My lack of girl friends. He admitted that he didn't have any close male friends, either. Said it was because of his family and because of his wanting to be a nurse. I wondered if a male and female could become best friends too, besides being attracted to each other. He almost read my mind. "I think we could be friends, even with dating and all, you know?"

By then we were sitting in the diner. The movie had been a comedy, and had been really good. The hamburgers were wonderful, sloppy and tasting slightly of onions on thick Italian rolls. Max's Uncle Dom had made them especially for us, and after the first platters came two more with French fries. "Your uncle is really neat. Is he Italian?"

"Yeah." Max smiled. Those white teeth got to me again. I wondered what it would be like to kiss him. "Talk about family, he's my mother's brother, but my father was English, Irish, Dutch and German, I think."

The subject about being friends didn't come up again until we were parked in front of my house. I'd offered to drop him off, but he said he would walk. I couldn't see the color of his fabulous eyes, but I felt the warmth of his arm around my neck. "Tessa, I really mean it. I want to be friends with you, but I want to..."

He kissed me then. It was terrific.

Chapter Eight

Waking up the next morning, I stretched in bed, thinking of Max. I wouldn't have been able to explain it to anyone, the feelings I was feeling. Dennis, back in Michigan, hadn't been able to make me feel like that. He'd made me feel like a real nerd for turning him down. Max made me feel like a treasure. Not a fragile treasure, like in a museum, but a living, breathing, responding, valuable person.

Mom shattered my thinking with a bang on my door. "Hey, sleepyhead, we're going to church, want to go?"

I was about to say no when I remembered my appointment with Dr. Boden at Sylvan Glade. I threw back my sheets and answered, "Okay. See you downstairs."

Why my sudden change of heart? Well, a prayer or two couldn't hurt if I was really going to keep that appointment.

Later, after my parents had left for a round or two of golf at the club, I dressed carefully in my white ducks, T and the smock which I had to iron. At the bottom of the ditty bag I found my old Girl Scout knife. I hadn't seen it in ages, but sort of remembered that Tim had needed it for something. I wished I could talk to Tim. I wished I could talk to someone. What would Max think about this? About my obsession with Stacy? Would friendship cover this?

The bug and I had to stop at the guarded gates of Sylvan Glade to get a confirmation of my appointment. Then I followed the winding drive to a huge, sprawling mansion, similar to ones built before the Civil War, except for the addition of wings flanking the original house. It was quite impressive, though.

Pillars rose to support the terrace that shadowed the porch below. Green shutters decorated the windows, and there were flowers everywhere. I passed a landscaped garden full of zinnias and delphiniums, and after parking in the almost empty lot, walked up the concrete walk past petunias, rudbeckia and marigolds. There were geraniums on the porch. Colorful flowers and no white ones. Dr. Waite had said he thought color was important to mental patients, and it looked as if Dr. Boden agreed with him.

She was colorful, too. Three inches taller than me, she wore her long, dark hair twisted back to a heavy bun at the nape of her neck, yet that was the only conservative thing about her. A slim, trim nurse had taken me to the office, and Dr. Boden had stood up. "Well, now, Tessa Murphy, I understand you're thinking about a career in psychiatry." Her words came out in a deep, throaty voice.

I said something, I'm sure, but her looks kind of shocked me. Her eye makeup was so loaded on that her thick glasses magnified a positive rainbow on her hooded lids. Her print dress under a white short-sleeved jacket would have brought a bull running.

"What makes you think you'd be good at it?" she asked harshly, sitting back down.

I figured that meant I could sit, too; I mean, go stand up like a child in front of a principal and recite the story of your life. Her question and the rough way she'd asked it made me nervous. "Er, I'm good with people..."

I went on with stuff I'd gotten from one of Dad's books on general psych, not that I'd read it recently, but having a good memory helps. The office walls were an almost hypnotic shade of shimmering blue, and that disoriented me, too. I wanted to get out of there, and away from Dr. Boden. How would a patient feel? "So, anyway, I'd love to see what you're doing here."

"You'd like a tour?" Again delivered in the harshest of tones. Although there were no cigarettes on the desk, and the ashtray looked clean, I could smell a stale scent of smoke. Maybe it was her perfume.

"Yes." I got to my feet at once. Opening the door to the hall, I took a deep breath stepping out. I was ready to scrap the whole thing and run.

She came after me. "You certainly are anxious."

"You bet," I said, getting myself under control.

And off we went. The immense indoor swimming pool was empty, and she informed me that on visiting days no one was allowed in swimming. However, the therapy of the water was absolutely unquestionable. Yes, there was an outdoor pool too, but it was used only on special occasions. Like what? No answer.

We moved on without my mentioning that the blue of the pool was exactly the same as the blue of Dr. Boden's office. And that it didn't seem very therapeutic to me.

The greenhouse was also empty. "The patients," Dr. Boden said, "love growing things. When they see their vegetables being served at meals and when they see the flowers in their rooms they are delighted."

"Oh." I poked a yellow rose. "How nice."

Tally ho, and we were off to the stables. No patients there either, but I was told how much they enjoyed tending to and riding the horses. Okay.

Getting antsy, I was led through the group therapy room, the physical therapy gym, the occupational therapy arts and crafts room, the game room with a pool table, chess and backgammon sets, and I was beginning to believe that an atomic war had taken place. Obviously, Dr. Boden and I were the only survivors.

Finally, I asked tentatively, "Do you think I could see some of the patients and their rooms?" Hadn't I worn the smock so as not to upset them?

She, just as tentatively, said, "I suppose so. But you mustn't say a word. They don't like strangers."

"Not a peep," I said, thinking how much I didn't like her. Just as well, I supposed; conning people one doesn't like is much easier.

Her espadrilles—purple, red and green—made slapping sounds as we crossed from the fun-and-games wing into the other. Visitors were arriving, and I checked them out. Some looked like they'd been dragged in by a wicked cat, and others appeared to be anticipating their visit. How would it feel to have a friend or relative here? Bad, awful, depressing? Yep, I thought so.

The Eye of the Storm

"The west wing is for nonviolent patients," Dr. Boden said, ignoring the visitors except for a smirk or two in their direction. "Which doesn't mean they are not peculiar, so be prepared for abnormal behavior. The second floor of the house proper is reserved for those with antisocial or psychotic behavior."

"Oh." So if Stacy was there she'd be on the second floor, not where Dr. Boden was leading me.

The rooms were gorgeous. Like settings from the soaps on TV, each was a different color and, besides beds, each had a sitting area. In a rose room, Dr. Boden declined a basket of fruit that a patient tried to give her. In a lavender room, a man was being ignored by his relatives as they caught each other up on the family news of the week. In yellow, a giddy man giggled at me; and in peach a woman yelled dirty words at Dr. Boden.

It was a relief, for a moment, to come to a white room. It held only a bed, one chair and several large, gory, religious pictures. The woman offered me a prayer book. When I shook my head politely, she yelled, "The Lord will smite you down!"

Cripes, I'd been to church that day! If only Dr. Boden hadn't told me to be quiet, I would have reported on the sermon.

"Dr. Boden," I said when we were in the hall again, "is it possible to see the psychotic patients? On the second floor?"

"My dear, Tessa." Dr. Boden was ready to dust me off. "Don't you think it would be too much of a strain?"

I'd noticed her constantly saying my name, checking my name tag too, as if trying to remember it. "A strain? Why, I don't think so. How can I get a true picture of what you're doing if I don't see everything? How can I possibly make up my mind about psychiatry?"

"I hate to say no to one who is so interested, but I think I must, Tessa."

"Dr. Boden." I lowered my voice into a confidential tone. "I didn't want to admit this before, but I have a cousin here. I just moved from Michigan last year, so we've never met. She's a niece of an aunt by marriage to my mother. You see, besides my desire to study psychiatry, I do qualify as a visitor."

Dr. Boden stared down at me witheringly. "And what is the name of this patient, Tessa?"

"Er, Stacy Harlon?"

Dr. Boden seemed relaxed as she said, "Oh, Stacy. Frankly, Tessa, I'm not sure. A visitor might do her some good—she never gets any."

"Doesn't Uncle David come to see her?" I acted surprised.

"No, no, she's sedated most of the time, and rather listless." Dr. Boden patted her hair for straying wisps. Not finding any, and seeing that I was still firmly planted in front of her, she added, "I'm afraid I still haven't gotten to that worm inside of her that turned her against her uncle. Is he a relative too?"

Panic. I couldn't remember what I'd said, except I'd called him Uncle David. "Yeah, he's more of a relative, I think, than she is. Families can be very complicated, don't you think?" I didn't wait for an answer. "Tell me, Dr. Boden, what medical school did you go to? I need some help deciding where to apply."

"Columbia," she said shortly.

For the first time I saw her off kilter. "Oh, did you intern in New York, too?"

The Eye of the Storm

"If you want to see Stacy, we'd better hurry. Visiting hours will be over before we know it."

Again I followed those espadrilles, wondering what on earth had put a bee up her bonnet. We climbed up a long, trailing staircase, and my feet sank into inches of carpet. The railing was carved mahogany. I could see Scarlett O'Hara floating down the stairs in a green dress, saying, "Fiddle-dee-dee."

On the second floor Dr. Boden paused by the nurse's desk. "This is Tessa Murphy. I'm going to take her in to visit Stacy for a moment. How is she today?"

The nurse was middle-aged, strong and husky. I could see muscles bulging under her thin blue uniform. "Quiet, thank goodness, Dr. Boden. Not at all like yesterday."

They chatted for a few minutes about some other patients while I stood, abandoned. The walls were aqua, the carpet avocado, the nurse's desk beige. It complemented the massive, intricately worked, wrought-iron gates that separated us from the loony bin. They were painted with a thick cream that reminded me of an old-fashioned ice cream parlor's decor. Huge potted trees were placed here and there, and there were more flowers blooming out of planters.

"We try to maintain a homelike atmosphere." Dr. Boden had remembered me. She had a large key in her hand which had come from a pocket of the jacket.

I was finally getting in! Being excited, I didn't notice Dr. Boden stopping until I trod on her espadrilles. "Jeremiah!" she said in that raspy voice. "What are you doing up here?"

The nurse, who had her head down at the desk checking some papers, looked up and also spied the shabby little man hiding behind three of the larger trees.

She got up immediately. "Dr. Boden, I'm sorry. I thought he'd left!"

"He's *never* supposed to be up here. You know that!" Dr. Boden was furious. She stalked the small man, grabbing around the trees until she found his sleeve. He shrugged his grungy khaki jacket off and went the other way, but she was too quick. She caught him by his shirt collar as he tried to get by her. He was so frightened that his eyeballs were rolling. I thought if they didn't stop they might roll away into tomorrow.

He gasped but didn't speak as Dr. Boden hauled him to the top of the stairs. She said, sweeter in tone than her grip implied, "Jeremiah, dear, you know you're not supposed to be up here. Now go on about your duties."

She flung him down the stairs. I held my breath, thinking the poor thing would end up at the bottom in a stupor. But no, he recovered, almost elegantly, and did a step dance until he had his feet firmly on the fourth step. He turned and looked up at Dr. Boden, his eyes blue and watery with tears. She flung the jacket into his face. "And don't come back."

Acting as if nothing had happened, Dr. Boden said to me, "Shall we go?"

Who was crazy there? The patients, me, or Dr. Boden? What a witch in any case.

Chapter Nine

You must know that your cousin Stacy has been through a difficult time." We were through the iron gate by then, and the floor was hushed; certainly not like any hospital I'd ever been in. There were no cries in the day, but maybe that thick carpet absorbed them.

"Yes, er, how many patients are up here?"

"Right now?" She appeared to be counting. "Not many, really. Stacy, of course, will be with us for a long time. The rest usually depart for other places that will take the criminally insane, after their families decide that there is no use paying the expenses to keep them in a homelike atmosphere. Your Uncle Dave made an agreement with us and the judge. He's so dear. He wanted Stacy to live in comfort."

Dave? An agreement? Dear? Oh, boy. The homelike atmosphere that Dr. Boden liked to emphasize did not mean that anyone was free to walk out of their rooms.

"We've reversed the locking principal here. I can go in, but the patients can't come out. I've found it much easier that way." Dr. Boden had lipstick on her teeth. I hadn't noticed it before, because she hadn't smiled before. I thought of a barracuda with blood on its teeth.

The Stacy who inhabited the pretty, ruffled, pink and green room plucked at the skirt of her flowered outfit, but didn't raise her head when Dr. Boden said, "Stacy, dear, your long-lost cousin is here. This is Tessa, Tessa Murphy."

I instantly felt remorse. Suppose I was so awfully wrong that I would do some damage?

"Hi," I croaked. My throat was terribly dry with anxiety. "I'm sorta a cousin by you of marriage, and I was in the neighborhood..." Dumb. Stacy didn't respond.

She rocked back and forth on the rocker without looking up, still worrying her skirt. I couldn't see her face clearly; her bright blond hair fell forward over her cheeks and cascaded down her blouse. I stepped closer and Dr. Boden put a restraining hand on my shoulder. It clutched at me, and I went on nervously, "Surely you remember Aunt Abigail?" I felt I had to put a name to the fictitious aunt. "She was married to an uncle of my mother's and used to talk about you all the time, and I thought since I live here now, I'd just pop in and see you. Don't you remember her? Aunt Abigail?"

At last she looked up and stared at me out of listless gray eyes. "Of course. Aunt Abigail. I remember everything. I'm so tired, though." Her face lowered again, and she seemed resigned to having an intruder as well as a phony Aunt Abigail.

"I think it's time we leave." Dr. Boden propelled me toward the door, her hand clawing into me. "That's enough for today. Stacy, perhaps your cousin will come back if you are nice to her."

"Thank you for coming," Stacy mumbled through a wisp of hair she started sucking. "I'm so tired."

Dr. Boden sped up her act and I was down by the front door in no time. "She must be kept sedated. Yesterday, she fooled a nurse into believing she'd taken her medication. Within hours she'd exploded into fits of anger. Practically all the furniture in her room had to be replaced after we got her calmed down."

"What medication is she on?"

"Really, Tessa, I have spent enough time with you, and Stacy's medication is of no concern to you." Dr. Boden opened the large front door to shoo me out. "Give my best to Dr. Waite." The thud of the door behind me said not to come back, either.

Whew. My sneaks trod along the walks, and I didn't notice the flowers. All that lying and scheming hadn't made a bit of difference. That Stacy must be the real Stacy. What the other one had been up to, I didn't know, or care at that point. I was ready to give up. No, I was not going to go back to the phone to play area-code roulette. Not me. Not ever again. I was going to keep my little nose to myself, and never stick it in anyone else's business.

The parking lot was almost full now, and I didn't notice a figure lurking behind a Cadillac until he called to me, "Hey, Missy lady. Missy lady, I wanna talk at you."

His jaw was loose and his words were sloppy, but I understood and waited for him to come out. Instead, he beckoned me to join him. I felt silly and scared at the same time. What did he want? Me? How insane was he? I froze on the other side of the car, saying, "You're

Jeremiah, aren't you?" He nodded and those rolling eyes went toward the sanitorium. "You stay there, and I'll stay here, and we'll talk."

"Like a game, Missy lady?" He grinned and gurgled something like a chuckle. "Is it a game—you wanna play hide to seek?"

"Not right now. We'll play later, okay?" He was disappointed. I leaned over the car, gripping the sun-hot lid. "You wanted to talk to me?"

"'Tis true." He nodded again and leaned over his side of the car. We were still about three feet away from each other, and he couldn't have grabbed me successfully from there, so I wasn't too afraid. His words were hard to form and came out with difficulty.

"They—" he rolled his eyes again "—they, she, that one in there—she ain't my Stacy. My Stacy gave me chocolates and my Stacy told me stories. I was loving her, and now she's gone and they, them in there, they, she won't tell me. Doctor is bad one; Stacy say she not even a real doctor."

Holy cow! "What? Then who is that in Stacy's room?"

Like a child, he whimpered, "Not Stacy. She be here before, one time. She be downstairs though, then. I don't know her name, 'xactly, but she was here!"

"Where's Stacy, then?" The car lid got hotter; so did I.

"I dunno." Tears cascaded down his cheeks. "She went out in the black day...."

"Jeremiah!" a shrill voice sounded, and I knew who it belonged to. She'd snuck up on us and was about two cars away.

As she sped by me and around the car, I yelled, "Dr. Boden, don't hurt him, he wasn't doing anything!"

The Eye of the Storm   91

She had him by the ear with one hand and the other was clutching both the khaki jacket and his shirt. She glared at me. "What was he saying?"

"Nothing much," I said limply, adding, "He wanted some candy, I think, chocolates, he said."

"Chocolates?" Dr. Boden repeated after me with disbelief.

"Chock-oo-lates," Jeremiah repeated after her, mauling the words with his now quivering jaw. His nose was running too. With the tears he was shedding, it was no wonder.

I couldn't stand it. "Let him go! He wasn't doing anything. Please! You're hurting him."

"Tessa," she said, her voice returning to its usual restrained harshness, "if you ever want to come back here again, I suggest you leave. You do not know how to handle patients, and I will never permit you to talk with them unless I am there." With that she released Jeremiah's ear, but not his jacket and shirt.

Since I hadn't been invited back anyway, I didn't have much to lose except, maybe, Stacy. Again. I retreated toward my car. "I'm terribly sorry, Dr. Boden, it won't happen again. I think I might send Jeremiah some candy though, surely that can't hurt?" She gritted her teeth instead of answering. I hated to leave, but what could I do to help?

The last I saw of Jeremiah he was being hauled up the front steps of the Southern-style mansion. I stopped in a shopping mall on the way home and spent too much on a large assortment of chocolate creams and nuts. Thinking that I'd had a hard day, I bought myself some, too.

I had the first delivered, and chomped thoughtfully on the second all the way to Lake Watson.

Pulling into the driveway, I tried to compose myself in case my parents were back. I dropped my cool act when I found an empty house and a note. They'd come back to change their clothes after the golf game and had gone to the Clarksons' across the street to swim and have dinner. I was invited to join them, and under other circumstances I'd have loved to. We're the only family on the block without a pool, and the Clarksons have the hugest.

At that point, though, I started sweating and shaking as if some tropical virus had gotten me. I figured it was only a reaction to Dr. Boden and the day's events, but I'd never had an anxiety attack before. I splashed some cold water on my face and wrists, downed a few glasses of it and felt a little better. When I sat at the kitchen table with a marker and scratch pad, I was still sweating but no longer shaking.

I tried to make a sensible list of what I'd seen and heard. I couldn't. Everything got jumbled. Like when I wrote:

1. Dr. Boden is a flake. Nonprofessional and vindictive.

I immediately added: "Jeremiah said that Stacy claimed Dr. Boden wasn't a real doctor." Then I wrote: "Check her credentials. How? With whom? The AMA?" Finally I got to the next point:

2. Stacy remembered Aunt Abigail who didn't exist.

So would I if I were loony tunes. Maybe she did have an Aunt Abigail anyway.

It went on like that. I finally gave up. I was getting nowhere fast. I toyed with the marker, noticing that it was green. "Hmm." I drew an eye, or as close to an eye as a nonartist could get, filled in the color of the iris, and said, "Hmm," again, getting a new notion.

I glanced at the wall phone to see if it would leap off its perch and come to me, helping me to make up my mind. Of course, it wouldn't. The big question was: Could I face another call to Todd Lewis? He wasn't real fond of me, but I had to do it.

As I rushed to the phone before I could change my mind, I thrust my aqua jacket off and threw it on the floor. Punching out the number, I decided to plunge right in. He answered and I rushed to head him off from hanging up on me. "Look, I'm sorry about the other call, but please listen to me. My name is Tessa Murphy and I'm not a reporter. I'm a Teen Volunteer at Lake Watson Community Hospital." He started to say something. "No, wait, hear me out!" I said. "I know you don't believe it, but I really think I saw Stacy at the hospital. I think she might have run away from the sanitorium..."

"Hold it!" he yelled. I stopped. Anyone would have; there was so much pain in his voice. "I called Dr. Boden yesterday," he went on. "And she assures me that Stacy is safe in Sylvan Glade. I don't know what you're trying to pull, but please stop it before I'm forced to call in the Lake Watson police. You could be charged with harassment, you know."

First a million dollars, now the police! I was silent, petrified. And through it all came the sinking feeling that Dr. Boden hadn't been fooled for a moment by my weak story about Aunt Abigail.

Not hearing anything, he added, "This is a sick joke, I'm sure, but I'm not making an empty threat."

I whined, "I, I, I was only trying to help." I hate whining. Staring down at the marker still in my hand, I changed my voice into one with a little more confidence. "Tell me, what color are Stacy's eyes? No, wait, stop, don't tell me. I'll tell you: If they are gray, she's at Sylvan Glade, but if they're green, she was at Lake Watson Community Hospital and needs our help. Which is it?" I knew that his answer could mean the police on my doorstep any moment. I waited, not taking a single breath.

He was a long time answering, then he asked, "What color hair?"

I'm an authority on coloring hair. I answered, "Both blond, but the one at Sylvan Glade was bleached and the one at Lake Watson was natural."

"Stacy tinted her hair. Stop bothering me." He sounded furious as he hung up. Again.

"Thanks a lot, Todd, and goodbye to you, too." I slammed down the receiver. In two seconds I wondered if I should call him back and explain in detail that there's a lot of difference between bleaching and tinting. I was sure the Stacy at Sylvan Glade had begun life as a brunette; however, the one at Lake Watson had probably just highlighted her already beige hair.

Totally depressed, I just stood there.

Chapter Ten

The depression was knocked out of me when the phone rang. It was my mother wanting to know if I'd come over to the Clarksons'.

Frankly, I could have used a swim right then. But I didn't want to face anyone. I chose to go upstairs and hurl myself into the shower, hoping I'd drown.

While the pellets of water cooled off my sweaty body, I wondered if Todd would have listened had I been older. Being a teenager does not help many situations, and mostly it's a big lousy drag. Maybe 'tweenagers would be a better word, because we're between everything. Either too old to be foolish, or too young to have smarts. Or vice-versa as far as I was concerned.

Back in my room, I kicked my bed, threw a few pillows around, stuck my tongue out at Mom's now-finished canna painting and picked up the only toy I have left from my childhood. My bear Tizzy. Most of the time he sits on a chair, ignored, but I needed him now. I didn't have anyone else to confide in.

Wait a minute! Maybe I did. All that talk about friendship the night before. It was worth a try. I called Max on my private line, carrying the phone over to the window to switch on the air conditioner. I was still sweating.

I clutched my towel around me as a cold blast came out and the phone was picked up at the other end. "Hi," I said to Max, feeling a warm glow fill me inside, even though there were goose bumps on my arms. "Can you come over for dinner? I need to talk to someone. My parents are out and it'll be just us. I really need to talk to someone."

"Someone?"

"You."

"Sure," he said. "And how are you?"

"Fine, sort of, and you?"

"Terrific. You want me to bring dinner—like a pizza?"

"Don't be silly. There's half a cow in the freezer."

"Wow. Where's the other half? She must be lonely without it." I laughed and he added, "I'll be there in half an hour, okay?"

"Okay." I glanced at my clock and saw that it was almost five-thirty. My phone call to Todd and then my temper tantrum had eaten away a lot of time.

I threw my hair up on my head in one swoop, pinning the mass into place. More than likely, with the kids in the house, Max was used to eating early, and I had to hurry.

Dressed in clean jeans and a red shirt, I raced down to the kitchen. "Whoa." I pulled myself up short. I didn't cook very well, and Max did. What was I going

The Eye of the Storm

to do? I was only familiar with the kitchen in passing, mostly passing in and out of it.

I took steaks out of the freezer and defrosted them in the microwave. In making the salad, I almost lost a whole bag of carrots down the garbage disposal, and when I tossed it, half landed on the floor. I washed it off and mixed it by hand.

Then I almost chopped a finger off while dicing garlic for the bread and wished I'd accepted the offer of pizza. When the doorbell rang, the bread was in a slow oven, the salad in the fridge, and I was a nervous wreck.

Max looked fabulous; big, strong, muscular and cute all at one time. Now that I liked him and didn't feel I had to put him down, he'd become familiar and adorable. He was holding a brown bag out to me, but I ignored it and leaned into him.

"Hey, what's up?" He held me close. "You're acting a little frazzled."

"I'm not real terrific in the kitchen," I mumbled into his shoulder. "In fact, I'm sort of lousy."

"Who cares? 'Sides, you're wearing my favorite perfume." He held me away and I looked up, frowning. I hadn't put on any perfume. He kissed me lightly on the lips, then took a hand and kissed my fingers. "Eau de garlic," he said, sniffing as he kissed.

Wow. Even with the sniffing, the kissing was the tingly sort. Plus, no one had ever kissed my fingers before. It was sweet and, well, sexy at the same time.

"Are you going to invite me in, or make me eat dinner on the stoop?"

"You can come in. What's in the bag?"

We walked through the living room as he said, "This'll cheer you up no end: I found part of the other half of that poor cow."

In the kitchen, I opened it. "Oh great, ice cream. Rocky Road. Guess you knew I'd forget dessert."

"Nope. I just can't come over to dinner without bringing something. What is wrong, Tessa? You're acting like a kitten with King Kong's fleas." His down-home country accent was laid on thicker than the rugs at Sylvan Glade.

"I'll tell you about it later, after dinner. I lit the grill outside and made some stuff, but I think you'd better do the steaks unless you like yours crispy."

Max peered down at the steaks while I put the ice cream in the freezer. "I think the patient needs some dressing, Doctor."

"What would you suggest, Nurse?" I went along with him and was comfortable doing it. A few weeks before, I'd thought for sure I'd fall for a doctor when I fell. Now, I was falling harder than an avalanche for a future nurse.

"Teriyaki?" Max asked hopefully.

"Terry who? Is he coming to dinner, too?" I went to the cupboard where Mom keeps all her spices and condiments, and found the right bottle.

"Yes." Max unscrewed the cap and sprinkled both sides of the meat. "He's the anesthesiologist."

As he rubbed the sauce into the meat, I said, "Thank goodness. I wouldn't want those poor things to feel any pain."

We ate on the patio, and I enjoyed watching him eat. Funny, I'd never thought about it before, but I'd always detested the way Dennis wolfed down his food, then burped for the world to hear. Jordan, on the other hand, was too proper; he always ate things like tacos with a knife and fork. Max tasted, enjoyed, and wasn't piggy or proper. Yep, I was falling. I suppose he could have eaten like a starving tiger and I'd still have had stars in my eyes.

When we were into the ice cream, he said, "Okay, what did you want to talk to me about?"

I took a spoonful from my dish and then put it back. "Well, speaking of rocky roads, I think I've been traveling on one. I don't know where to begin, though."

"Sounds serious. Maybe start and I'll catch up?"

I would have preferred it to be dark. It would have been easier to talk if I hadn't kept watching his face for disbelief. It was also pretty difficult to admit what an accomplished liar I'd become. My face was downcast, my eyes on my lap as I finished.

There wasn't a word from him until I lifted my head to meet his gaze. Then he said, "I wish you'd told me about this before. Didn't you think it might be dangerous?"

"No. I didn't know that Todd had called her—how could I?"

"But if it's a conspiracy, well, right. Do you really think that Dr. Boden let you in to see Stacy *because* Todd Lewis called her?"

"Don't you see? She let me in to see Stacy so that I'd think that Stacy was there."

"And yet you think she's not the right Stacy?"

"Todd said she had green eyes. The one in the sanitorium had gray eyes."

"Some people think I have green eyes; some people think they're blue. Green and gray can be like that, don't you think?"

Yipes. He was right. As the sun dimmed, his eyes were more green than blue. "Okay, hotshot, who was the Stacy in the hospital?"

"Maybe *she* was a reporter. Maybe her name really was Stacy. Maybe she wants to write the book that Mrs. Terry wants to write. Maybe she got confused. Isn't that possible?"

"That's a lot of maybes," I retorted, irritated. Falling in love was one thing, but being grilled like steaks was another. I was flushed, hot, sweaty, and the mass of melted chocolate in front of me wasn't too appealing. "What about the phony doctor on the stairs?"

"You're the only one who says he was a phony." Max leaned back in his chair. I noticed *he'd* finished his ice cream.

I resented that, as well as his attitude. "So what? Now you're acting like a lawyer. Believe me, I prefer the nurse."

He came forward immediately and took my hands in his. "Sorry. Okay, why do you think he was a phony?"

I sighed. "You'll think this as impossible as the rest, but he was wearing a surgical mask..."

"Oh," he interrupted me. We both knew that outside of the operating room, a doctor does not wear a mask unless he's visiting a contagious patient, and then he puts on a freshly sterilized one. "In all that heat and humidity? Must have been hard for him to breathe. Maybe in all the confusion?"

"Another maybe?" I knew what he meant, though. During the excitement of the hurricane, there might have been several doctors, and nurses, who'd forgotten they had masks on. The masks became, to them, part of their anatomy.

Max kept holding my hands. "So, if she was a reporter, maybe he was her editor, oh forget it. That's stupid. He could have walked in the front door. I was thinking that she could have gotten out of bed to make

The Eye of the Storm 101

the phone call, fallen and hit her head, then her friend comes along and hoists her back, but that doesn't make sense. Why would he be dressed like a doctor?"

"See?"

"I see." He nodded. "The thing is—what are we going to do now?"

"We?" I asked hopefully.

"Yeah, we. Why not?"

"Makes sense to me," I said, relieved. Leaning forward, I kissed him to prove it.

We broke apart, both of us feeling the moment deeply. I know I did, and was sure he did too when he picked up my bowl of melted chocolate and said, "I'll get you some more."

When he came back the bowl was piled high. We both dug our spoons in, and he said, "I'm not saying to stop what you're doing, but I don't know whether it's right or not."

"If I'm not right, at least maybe I can expose Dr. Boden for what she is, a rotten person."

He teased, "Another maybe?"

"Nope." I licked my spoon. "Not as far as I'm concerned. She's sadistic, I'm telling you."

"I believe you. Did she have any degrees framed and hanging on the wall?"

"Nope. What does that mean?"

"There was an article recently in some medical journal about checking up on doctors and psychiatrists—first thing you look for is degrees on the wall."

"Ha! And she fudged when I asked her about medical school."

"Then, you're supposed to call the American Psychoanalytic Association if there's any doubt," he went on. "I'll do that. You've got enough phone bills to cope with."

"Wow." I grinned. "I knew there was a reason I liked you."

"Yep." He grinned back, shoving some ice cream into my mouth. When we kissed it was cold, warm and delicious.

My parents came home about ten minutes later, but luckily Max and I were in the kitchen, cleaning it up. After some good-natured teasing about my having cooked dinner, they went to bed and I walked Max outside to his motorbike. We took a long time to say good-night.

The last thing he said was, "Don't do anything by yourself. I'll be happy to back you up."

Chapter Eleven

While I was sipping my coffee the next morning and Mom was buttering a large Danish, she said, "I have to go into Houston later, to drop off some little paintings at Hodges, and pick up a huge check."

"You want my help carrying it?" I asked, hoping for another answer.

"Nope, spending it." She winked. "We can get some big print shirts, a couple more skirts for you and some dresses, maybe?"

That was the answer I wanted. After all, I couldn't keep wearing the same outfit every time I went out with Max, and it looked like that might be quite a bit. "Great."

"Good. A white skirt and jacket, and some of those bright colored undershirts. I think you need some shorts too, and your bathing suits are a disaster."

Right then I remembered Mrs. Terry. I had to pick up those clippings! "When, what time?"

"Some new makeup. I want to find exactly the right eyeshade for you. It has to have mocha in it, of course. And I think if you got a little more sun, a bronzer blush would be better than that sissy pink—" She was off into her own world, studying my face as if it were a blank paper to be painted.

She had me salivating and torn between my need for those newspaper stories and my need to impress Max on our next date. *"What time?"* I practically yelled.

"Hmm? Oh, around twoish, I guess. After shopping, we could have an elegant dinner at the Galleria." She came back to earth with a slight jolt. "Why? Are you going someplace?"

"The library," I said quickly. "I, er, have a book due."

"You have plenty of time." She checked her watch. "It's only ten now, but since you're going out, would you pick up some stuff for me?" Without my answer, she got up to get the pad by the phone, sat back down and began scribbling with the same green marker I'd used the day before. Inside I winced; outside I looked the picture of a dutiful daughter, anxious to please her mother.

"There." She tore off the paper and handed it to me. "And puh-leeze, don't forget the Lake Watson Cleaners. I got a notice from them saying they're closing tomorrow."

"Them too? Boy, that Lake Watson Shopping Mall is a waste."

"Yeah, well, they shouldn't have built it on that hillock. And they can't compete with the bigger ones out on the highway. But I've heard that some enterprising

The Eye of the Storm 105

cookie is going to build a disco there, with a bowling alley and a roller-skating rink!"

"Perfect!" I liked that idea. Max and me dancing, skating!

I got away about an hour later, walking into the library on hesitant feet. Right then all I could think about was Mrs. Terry, and how she might have had second thoughts.

Nope. She saw me sneaking up to her desk and beamed at me with a broad smile. She resembled a novice spy giving out state secrets from the U.S. to Russia as she handed me a large envelope and whispered, "There you go. I hope it helps. Don't forget me."

"I won't," I promised. I wouldn't ever, I thought. Even if it all turned out to be a flea in a beehive, I'd never forget her, and I'd make it up to her somehow. "Thanks, really, thanks."

"No problem." She was looking very excited as I left.

I flew the bug over to the diner, thinking that Max might like to see the clippings, but he was so busy with prelunch duties he didn't have much time. When he could sit down for a minute, he brought me a pecan roll and coffee. "Don't tell me you made this, please don't tell me that." I sighed, expecting him to say he did. It was a mountain of puffed glaze and pecans.

"I didn't." Max sipped his coffee. "My mother did. That's where I learned how to do what I can do, but she's a real baker. She's got her own business. You should see the kitchen at our house. What are these?"

"The clippings." Max was reading them swiftly. "What do you think?" I asked between heavenly bites.

"In a word, wow!" He took the nearest clipping. "'Local Girl Judged Insane.' That's a heavy trip." He read some of the text out loud, but had to put it down when his uncle called from the kitchen. "Got to go. My shift is from four to eight at the hospital. Can I come over after?"

Grumpily, I admitted to my date with Mom.

Max took my hand. "No big deal. How about if I stop by after your shift tomorrow? If your parents are around, we could go out and read these over together."

"Terrific," I answered, thinking how weird it was that I had to turn down a date with Max in order to go and buy clothes to go out with Max.

He walked me out to the bug and kissed me lightly on the forehead, then on both cheeks, and then my hand. Then my other hand was turned over and I got kissed on my palm. He studied the palm after he'd kissed it and said, "I see a dark man with blue-green eyes who will always be in your future."

"Wow," I said. "But can he bake a rhubarb pie?"

"You bet." He kissed me on the lips and let me get into the bug, but waved while I was driving away. All that gave me a good feeling, and I breezed through Mom's chores with a smile on my face and a "Have a good day" on my lips. Usually, or at least when I first came to Texas, the sunny greeting annoyed me, but not that day. I wished everyone could have as good a day as I figured mine would be. Wrong, again.

After I'd bought some needle-nosed pliers and an extension cord at a hardware store in the mall near the highway, I saw the brown Toyota for the first time. It was parked in the slot next to the bug, and I think the only reason I noticed it was because it was all smeared with mud, including the license plate.

I checked out the bug and thought it could use a wash, but dumped the hardware in the back seat and went on to another parking place nearer the supermarket. One of the things on Mom's list was to buy some frozen dinners for Dad. To give him a choice because we were going to feast in Houston that night. Dad does not cook, and as I was picking up and rejecting things, I thought about Max. Lord, leave him alone for one night and I bet he'd feed the starving children in Ethiopia. I dwindled my selections down to three and hoped Dad would be happy, got some paper towels, and filled all the other needs on the list, then went out to the bug.

Funny, the brown Toyota was right by my side again, looking even more filthy. There was a car wash at the end of the long parade of stores and endless lanes, so I drove the bug over, thinking that there might be a dozen brown Toyotas around Lake Watson, Texas, that were filthy.

I was slushed, brushed and wiped, but pulling out of the car wash onto the highway, I saw the brown Toyota again. It hadn't been washed and seemed to be following me. "Must be your imagination, Murphy," I told myself, checking in the rearview mirror.

There was a Burger King on my right, one that I had to go through some trouble to get to. I wasn't hungry, not after that pecan thing I'd eaten, so I ordered a Coke and sat at a table to watch outside. Sure enough, there was the brown Toyota. Out in the parking lot, very near the bug but not beside it. I dumped half the Coke, feeling queasy. I'd heard a lot of news stories about teenage girls disappearing. Cripes! There were serial murderers out there! At the time, I never thought about the Stacy thing; I only thought that a rapist might be following me. *Only?* I certainly didn't want the guy to follow me home, and I had another stop to make. If I saw the car in the almost-abandoned, soon-to-become-a-hot-spot shopping mall in Lake Watson, then, maybe, I'd have reason to be worried.

Sure enough, after I'd parked the bug and was inside the cleaners, I saw the brown Toyota cruising as though looking for a parking place. There were tons of them; a good three-quarters of the stores had closed. "Uh, could I use your phone?" I asked the elderly man who handed me Mom's dry-cleaned stuff. "It's sorta important."

"Love to, girlie, but we's closing and the phone, it been done took out. We's got a new address, ya know?" He handed me a card that couldn't help me, but I took it, automatically. "You wanta phone, therse one 'cross the lot, a payer."

"Oh," I said. Then I tried to engage him in some conversation. "So you're moving?" I glanced at the card. "Oh, the Clute Shopping Mall, that's kind of far away, isn't it?"

"Mebbe, mebbe not."

That was it. The conversation had come to an end. The old man turned away from me, and I was left with the clothes and my panic. Picking up the plastic-wrapped clothes, I went slowly to the door, but not seeing the brown Toyota still cruising cheered me up. I told the old man to have a good day, and stepped out into the bright sun.

Nope. No Toyota around. Only my bug, two other cars and a large truck parked at the dead end of the lot. I stowed the clothes in the back seat and looked at my watch. Yipes! It was alarmingly close to two. I could be home in eight minutes, but then I'd have to change since we were going out to dinner. Figuring I'd better let

The Eye of the Storm

Mom know I was on my way, I crossed the parking lot to the pay phone in an open kiosk.

While I was talking to Mom, and she was saying it was okay, but please hurry, however not too much because I shouldn't have an accident or get a ticket, I cased the parking lot some more. No shoppers, no strollers; the place was creepy.

I hung up, and immediately heard the gunning of a motor! The brown Toyota came out from behind the truck and sped straight toward me. I screamed and ran!

There was a sidewalk and I stuck to it, afraid to cross the lot and thinking the car wouldn't come up on it. Wrong! It did.

I froze for half a second, my breath caught in my throat, gasping out, "Stop!"

When the car was a fraction away from running me down, I forced myself to somersault away and rolled down a grassy slope below the lot. I landed, arms and legs sprawled, at the bottom of a gully. Daisies and Queen Anne's Lace grew with wild abandon there. How could they when I was so scared?

I lay in a motionless heap, shutting my eyes. If that maniac came down to check on me, I'd figure out a way to fight him off.

There was silence except for some flies buzzing around me, until I heard an engine start up. I breathed, but didn't move, not for another few minutes. Then I untangled myself slowly. My jeans were grass stained and my hair a mess.

When I was safely in the bug, I realized I should have called the police from the pay phone, but I couldn't wait to get home. What if he came back? It had to be a he, I rationalized, although I hadn't seen the driver. Women maniacs must go after young boys.

Women? Oh, no! I'd come to a stop at a red light and realized then that it might be connected to Stacy. Maybe Dr. Boden had decided to discourage me, so maybe it had been a woman after all. "Mebbe, mebbe not." I repeated what the old man had said through clenched teeth. In any case, if I told the truth to Mom and called the police from home, I'd be in deep trouble if I mentioned that theory. The poo-poo would hit the fan for sure, and I'd never get a shopping spree again ever.

I was feeling myself all over for bruises and lumps when the car behind me beeped impatiently. The light had changed, and I jumped in my seat, feeling a slight crick in my neck.

The first thing I did was check my rearview mirror. The car behind me was green, thank goodness, and I shifted gears to speed through the light before she beeped again.

I was home in minutes, still frightened as I pulled into the driveway. Had the driver meant to kill me? No, I thought not. Maybe he/she had just wanted to scare me off the Stacy thing? It had almost succeeded.

"You'd better hurry," Mom said as soon as I went into the house. "I told Douglas we'd be there at 3:30. You know how he fusses."

She didn't even notice my frazzled condition as she took the plastic-wrapped clothes. "Sorry," I mumbled, glad she didn't. "Ten minutes," I added, racing up the stairs.

Mom hates to keep Douglas Hodges waiting. He's done more for her reputation as an artist than she'd ever thought possible. Back in Michigan, she'd shown at a local gallery where the owner had taken fifty percent of the selling price and kept treating her like she was a silly housewife, not the pro she is. Douglas takes thirty-five percent and fawns all over her. Plus, he's hyped her so much that a painting of hers only stays in his gallery for two days before it's sold.

I made it on the nose. Even managed a quickie shower, and then threw on the same outfit I'd worn on my first date with Max. I put on some makeup in the car and brushed out my heavy hair, ignoring the crick in my neck.

The crick got worse when I kept twisting my head around to look back for a brown Toyota. Finally, I angled the rearview mirror outside the passenger seat to reflect perfectly all the cars behind us, and started to relax.

Mom didn't. No matter what time of day, and most of the night, traffic streams toward Houston and away, on three-lane highways, with underpasses and overpasses a driver has to pay attention to. Mom gripped the wheel and gave all her attention to her driving. As for me, with the miles dropping by between us and Lake Watson, and no brown Toyotas around, I felt safer and safer.

After a long stop at the art gallery, we went on to the Galleria, the most fantastic shopping center in the world. It's attached to a hotel, and people come from everywhere to stay there and shop to their heart's content.

When I stopped in front of jeans, Mom pulled me along. When I wanted new sneaks, she bought me heels. "What if I trip?" I asked.

"It's time you got used to them, and I think sneakers give a false sense of security anyway. And you have such nice legs. You should show them off more." She stopped in front of a rack of short skirts.

"Oh Mom, don't you think that's sort of antifeminist?"

"Do you think so? Is the store wired? Is Betty Friedan listening?"

I choked up with laughter. "Okay, one short skirt, but could I get some long shorts, too?"

"Deal."

We went on like that. There were several dresses added to our purchases, one that I couldn't resist. A knockabout thing with big pockets and a tiny teddybear pattern.

We had lobster tails for dinner at an elegant Tiffany-lamped place with lots of wood carvings and lots of Houston's big spenders. On the drive home both Mom and I were yawning, and it was after eleven when we pulled into the garage, passing the bug in the driveway.

I hugged her good-night, thanking her for all my new clothes. "You didn't buy anything for yourself," I added.

"I didn't? Guess we'll have to make another assault on the Galleria next week."

"Terrific." I waved as I went up the stairs.

Outside my door, I had a sense of foreboding. It was silly, I thought, hitting the light switch and illuminating the room. Then I got a chilly feeling that someone had been there. Nothing to pinpoint my suspicions except that my bear, Tizzy, had been moved. He usually sat on a chair, neglected, until I needed him to cuddle with. Now he was upside down on the bed. I picked him up and said, "I got a dress that has bears like you all over it." I unpacked the boxes and bags, wishing he could talk. I hadn't left him on the bed like that, had I?

One of my windows was open, and I looked outside. There was a tree that I'd never thought about being

The Eye of the Storm

there before. It would give good access to my premises. Scared, I closed the window and turned on the air conditioner. I went back and locked the other window.

Still not exactly happy, I sat myself down at my desk, inserted paper in my typewriter and started a letter to Tim. When I got to describing the clippings, I reached for them automatically and remembered they were still in the bug. Outside. In the driveway.

The house was very quiet as I went downstairs. I flitted across the front yard, my keys in my hand. On my own turf I wasn't frightened; the neighborhood was safe. I was in and out of the bug in seconds, clutching the envelope to me, and headed back to the front door when I heard, "Tessa. Tessa."

My first thought was an unreal one, that Max was in the bushes somewhere. The voice hadn't sounded all that threatening.

"Tessa!" Then it did. It was low and menacing.

I ran for the stoop and clambered up it. I heard a final, horrible "Tessa!" as I slammed the door and locked it.

Mom came out of the back bedroom. She said sleepily, "What was that? Who's there?"

"Me," I admitted. "I forgot something in the car. I think there's a prowler outside."

"Uh-oh." Mom flipped on the switch by the door, and the hall was flooded with light. She blinked about three hundred times in rapid succession. "What did you see?"

"Nothing, really. I just heard a voice calling 'Tessa, Tessa!'"

"You didn't imagine it. No, of course you didn't. You're very levelheaded. I guess I'd better call the police."

First I have great legs, now I'm levelheaded. How long had she kept these opinions to herself, I wondered. Anyway, then Dad came out. He was all tousled with mussed-up hair. "Tessa was attacked outside," Mom told him.

"Well, it wasn't an attack, exactly." I tried to explain.

"Attacked!" Dad was the epitome of the angry parent.

The police came and I admitted that it wasn't the attack Dad had told them about on the phone. They searched for a prowler and told my parents that no one was there, ignoring me. Dad scratched his head, anxious to go back to sleep, and Mom hugged me a lot. Thank goodness nobody noticed the file of clippings lying on the hall table. Going back upstairs, I felt stupid again. Had there been a brown Toyota? Had I taken a tumble? Had there been a voice?

I got the answer a few minutes later. My parents had been so sleepy they wouldn't have heard my private phone ring even if it had rung like the bells in Lake Watson's biggest church. I did, though.

"Today was a warning," a rough voice said when I answered. "You're not safe, you know. We can go wherever you go. Did you see your bear on the bed? That was another warning. And did you hear our voice calling tonight? No matter where you are, or what you do, we'll get you if you don't leave it alone. Now, leave it be, or you'll be dead."

I gasped, "Leave what be?"

"Don't act stupid. We know you're not. You're too smart for your own good. And if you call the police again, or tell anyone about this, you're gonna be history."

The line went dead and I dropped the receiver into the cradle as if it were too hot to handle. I was sweating, chilled and scared, again. Too hot to handle? That was such an apt phrase, I felt like writing it down to remind me of the rough-tough voice on the phone and his message. I was sure I should quit while I was behind and still alive.

Chapter Twelve

Mrs. Nettles greeted me with doom and gloom. "Oh, you're early, perhaps that's just as well. Your father wants to see you in his office. Now!"

"Oh," I said. Then took off.

Stupid me. As I ran across the complex to Dad's office, I never thought about the Stacy thing. I only thought that some disaster had happened to Mom or Tim. I was breathless as I ran past Dad's receptionist, and nurse, to Dad's open door. "What is it? I just left Mom. It isn't Tim?"

"No, it's you." Dad slapped his open palm on the desk, and I saw how furious he was. "Shut the door." I did, and he went on, "I can't imagine what has gotten into your head. Have we been too lenient with you? My father used to believe in a quick kick in the fanny if I didn't behave. I hated it, but now I wonder if that isn't the answer."

The Eye of the Storm

"What's the question?" I asked more glibly than I felt. I eased my unkicked fanny onto the chair next to the desk. Perched there, with only the leather padding between me and his foot, I felt guilty. I knew I'd been found out.

"Don't get smart with me, young lady." For once his glasses were in their proper place, like they'd been glued on. "I've been on the phone half the morning finding out about your little crusade." My mouth formed an oh, but I didn't say it. "The first call was from Dr. Waite. That one didn't make much sense at first because he was so angry, and I hadn't the least notion what he was talking about. But then I got it: it seems that a Dr. Jocelyn Boden from Sylvan Glade had called him, saying that she'd checked with a—" he paused to look at a notebook spread open on his desk. He punched it with a finger and read off, "A David Jennings who said you were not a relative at all to a—" another look at the notes "—Stacy Jennings Harlon who, it seems, is being kept at Sylvan Glade because she's believed to be criminally insane. Dr. Waite went on for some time about my being so unprofessional as to instill in a child of mine the belief that she can use my contacts to accommodate some morbid curiosity."

"It wasn't curiosity!"

"Shut up." He slapped the desk again. In all my life he'd never spoken to me like that. Never. Sometimes he'd been stern, sometimes too busy to listen. Not this. I was in shock.

"That one of my colleagues would be so upset with a child of mine is unforgivable. Then—" another brief glance down "—a Todd Lewis called from San Francisco. It seems that you have been bothering him with endless phone calls."

"Just two," I whispered.

"Two is quite enough. He is talking harassment charges against you."

I wanted so badly to tell my side of the story that I opened my mouth and then was cooled off by his stare.

"No, I don't want to hear it. I know you well enough to know that you thought you had some good reason for this, probably that this Stacy was our missing patient, but I will not tolerate you going off to investigate like this. I told you the hospital didn't want to get involved. How will it look if Todd Lewis does call the police? Files charges? Don't you think the newspapers would find out? Don't you think they'd play up the missing patient angle? How would it look to the public?"

I was shaking, inside and out. "I didn't think about that."

"No, you didn't think about anything." He crossed his arms on the desk, angling his head forward. "And who is going to pay the phone bills to Alberta, Canada, as well as San Francisco and the other places?"

"I will," I whispered. "How did you..."

"After Mr. Lewis called, I checked with the phone company to see what else you'd been up to."

Redness mottled my cheeks. It was air-conditioned in the office but I might have been smack-dab on the equator the way I felt.

"Oh, Tessa. Do you need attention so desperately? And that business last night! Hearing voices. I feel like calling the police and apologizing for bringing them out like that."

"It happened, Dad! It did!"

"What did we do wrong? I would have said you were happy—well, never mind." Dad proceeded to the sentence, since he'd already condemned me without a trial. "Until we can get this problem of yours straightened out, there will be no more TeeVees, no more dates, your phone will be taken out of your room and your car privileges suspended until I decide what else to do."

"But the hospital work is important." I tried to salvage one thing, anyway.

It didn't budge him. "Yes, I agree. It has been important to you. You, however, have not been important enough to it to merit your continuing. One has to wonder what other kind of trouble you'll stir up in your present condition. And *if* you still want to be a doctor, you'll have to learn about following orders. Now, I've talked to your mother, and the first order you have to follow is to go straight home, turn over the car keys to her and go to your room."

Angry now, I stood and snapped, "Yes, sir! Anything else, sir!"

"Get out of here, before I remember how my father used to kick my fanny."

I was out and away before he'd half risen from his chair.

I was still angry as I started the bug up, but tears were pouring down my cheeks. Couldn't he have listened for a second? I'd heard he'd been so tough on students back in Michigan that they'd called him, "Old Iron Head." I'd never believed it before. Was that why Jordan had been so nervous when he'd thought I'd report his nasty behavior?

Had Mom ever seen him like that? No, I thought not. She had her own temper and would have booted him out of the house. Besides, his biggest complaint had been about my unprofessional behavior. I should have told him that I'm not a professional yet, I should have.

I should have—oh, what was the use. I was grounded as solidly as a rock.

Not yet, I wasn't. Not until I got to the house. What would a trip to Max's diner take? Another few minutes, and who was timing me? Even if Dad called Mom to tell her I was on my way, I could say I ran into traffic. Or I could even say I couldn't see the road because I was crying so hard. Which was almost true. I made the turn, pulled into the diner and ran in wildly.

It was crowded. Max was busy taking orders behind the counter. He spotted me and my condition. "Hey, what's wrong?"

"I have to talk to you, stat!"

Hospital talk, but it worked. He shoved his orders into the slot leading to the kitchen behind him, came around, grabbed my arm and took a waitress off the floor to deal with the counter. Outside, he put his arms around me. "What is it?"

I put my arms around him, too. He was big, muscular and mighty reassuring. Finally, I pushed him away, looked up and told him all. He reached into his jeans pocket and pulled out a hankie, all clean and smelling of fabric softener. "Blow," he said.

I did and was glad to. My shoulder bag was back in the bug and had lots of messy paper hankies inside. I don't think there's anything more satisfying then being mopped up by someone with a clean, large cloth. "I told you not to take any chances," he said.

"I didn't! Since when is going to the dry cleaners taking a chance?"

"I see what you mean. I have to tell you, I spent about an hour on the phone yesterday with the biggest library in Houston, tracking down Dr. Boden's credentials. Not only is she not a psychiatrist, she only has a masters in psych and doesn't deserve to be called doctor at all."

"How could she possibly get that job?"

"Shhh. Actually, the library only took a half hour, the other half hour was very well spent talking to a clerk in the county registrar's office. Guess who owns Sylvan Glade?"

"David Jennings," I spit out.

"Bingo."

"How'd you get that information? They talked to you?"

"My Mom bakes, you know? And it just so happens that one of her big customers for lemon custard cream pie is a judge. Who just happens to be a big wheel—et cetera, et cetera."

"Oh, Max. What would I do without you? Cripes, what am I going to do without you? I can't see you, I can't even talk to you!"

Max's uncle came outside looking for him then, but Max kissed me anyway. "The way I feel about you is I'll wait until you can reenter society. How long could it take? Two years, three? I'll wait, I'll be true-blue. From time to time, I'll bake you a cake and pass it through your window."

"Make sure it has a file in it so I can saw through the bars."

"You got it."

All in all, the visit had taken only five minutes, and Mom wasn't standing by the door. As a matter of fact, she was in her studio, next to Dad's study, savagely rendering a rose. A very large rose; a hot-pink rose. Not her usual style. "Make sure you get the thorns in, too," I said from the doorway.

"I'd like to stick a few thorns into you," she said, not looking up. "Put your keys on the table by the door and go to your room."

"I'm sorry," I said, telling another lie. I wasn't sorry at all, except that I'd gotten caught. But who could know that a couple of pretty terrific parents could become tyrants at the drop of a hat?

"I'm hungry."

"I'll bring you up a tray later."

"Bread and water? I don't suppose I could have one last phone call to order some pizza?"

"Cute," she said through clenched teeth. "Your phone has already been unplugged. Get upstairs, now!"

What a bum rap. I sat on my bed with my stomach rumbling. Would the world ever hear from Tessa Murphy again? I thought about Stacy then. The one who'd gotten me into this mess. Was I angry at her? No. But I had more reasons then ever to find her. I had to prove I was right.

Mom came up with a tray about ten minutes later. It didn't look like she was too mad at me. Grilled cheese with bacon and tomatoes, a soda and some spice cake. "I called Max to let him know you can't see him tonight," she said. "He's such a nice boy, I don't know what he sees in you."

"Maybe he likes criminals."

She spurted a tiny laugh, then sat on the bed next to me. "I don't know what to say to you. You've always been so sensible, now this. Your father thinks we have to find a shrink for you."

A shrink? Lord have mercy. With my luck I'd end up in nondoctor Boden's clutches. "Mom, I had reasons for what I did."

The Eye of the Storm 123

"I suppose you thought you did, but you went about it in the wrong way. Why, if you used my contacts at Hodges for some reason, I'd be just as p.o.'d as your father."

I couldn't think of any reason I'd do that, unless I thought Stacy was being kept in the basement of the gallery. Of course, that was one place I hadn't looked.

"Better eat before it gets cold. Just leave the tray outside, and if you need anything, holler."

"Am I allowed to go to the bathroom, or should I plan on wetting my bed?"

"You do that and you're in real trouble." Mom smiled a real, honest smile as she left.

I felt lonely again. I got up from the bed and sat at the little table by the window, eating and thinking rotten thoughts. Mom hadn't taken out my small TV, so I turned it on and indulged myself in soap operas. They had more trouble than I! I couldn't imagine how they'd lived through the things they had.

They reminded me, though, that I hadn't looked through the copies of clippings Mrs. Terry had given me. Thank goodness *she* hadn't called Dad, too.

I made notes as I read every word, scanning the photos again. The television hummed in the background, and truthfully, I didn't feel so locked up as I had at first. I guess everyone had to have quiet time to think. I heard Dad come home and wondered if he'd come up to say hello. He didn't. Mom brought my dinner tray up, and I managed to hide the articles before she saw them. She had a mischievous grin on her face as she put the tray on the table. "I talked him out of the shrink," she whispered, but left quickly.

Dinner was round steak, mashed potatoes and gravy. There was a salad and more spice cake spritzed with real whipped cream. And there was a CARE package of cookies and pretzels, in case I got hungry later. At least the food in my prison was good. I wished I could call Max and tell him. Heck, I wished I could call Dial-A-Prayer at that moment.

It was getting to me again. I had the books, I had the TV, I had the clippings, and I got to go to the bathroom. The tree outside looked good. I'd never had an occasion to use it, but now it could mean freedom. Except where would I go?

That answer came to me in a dream. I'd dozed off after reading the clippings over and over. It was a light sleep, and both Stacys were laughing at me, telling me they'd played a trick on me. I did not find it amusing.

The interesting part of the dream was that they were both in the old Jennings mansion. The one in the papers. Sure enough, when I struggled out of their peals of laughter, I blinked and looked down. And there was the clipping with the floor plan of the house right on my lap.

Funny about dreams. Sometimes they are so real it's disgusting, but sometimes they provide answers. The mansion was the one place I'd never thought of!

That was supposing that Stacy had not left the hospital under her own steam. Surely though, if she had she'd be in San Francisco by now, or at least have phoned Todd. It was Tuesday! Almost six days since she'd disappeared.

And why had Todd waited until today to call Dad? My first call to him had been Friday morning, but I hadn't given my name until the second on Sunday. Why did he wait a day and a half?

"Oh." The picture was getting clearer and clearer. It was a setup all the way around. "First spend a day scaring the dickens out of the little brat—me—then use her parents to put the clamps on her."

I was pretty sure Todd Lewis and Dr. Waite were innocent victims, as I was. Well, my jury was out on Todd, though. If he really cared about Stacy, he would have believed me!

I studied the floor plan for a while, not sure I had the nerve to add breaking and entering to my life of crime. The alleged attack had taken place in the study, which was between the library and the billiard room. The kitchen, formal dining room, breakfast nook were in the back, where there was also a parlor and morning room. Then a huge living room. What the heck was the dif between a parlor and living room? "And what the blankety-blank is a morning room?"

Maybe I wasn't born to know. I mean, one would have to be raised in such a place to know where and what everything was. The article only covered the first floor, too. It mentioned the second as having a ballroom and a gallery of paintings. The third was where the bedrooms were, and the fourth was where the servants had been quartered.

Most of the servants had been dismissed after Old Man Jennings had died, though. Why? I tapped my pen on my teeth. David Jennings said his niece had tried to kill him. David Jennings owned Sylvan Glade. Stacy had been committed before her eighteenth birthday when she would have collected millions. David Jennings was in control of those millions. Made sense to me. And where better to hide the real Stacy than in her own house?

Let the doped-up phony Stacy pass for the real one for years and years. I bet the phony one didn't have any close relatives. I bet it had been easy for Dr. Boden to pull the old switcheroo, except for Jeremiah, which explained her anger toward him.

Confident that I now had the answers, I turned off my light and slept with the clippings, setting my inner alarm clock to wake me up before daylight.

Chapter Thirteen

Dressed in my oldest jeans, an army-green T-shirt and my filthiest sneaks, I went down the tree at 4:30 a.m. My trusty Girl Scout knife was in my back pocket, and I'd taken a pencil flashlight from Tim's room to help along the path to the front of the house.

The bug sat there in the driveway looking squat and dark. I had locked it, but I'd also taken the extra keys from Tim's desk. Something my parents hadn't thought about. If push had come to shove, I also had been taught by my big brother to pick a lock and hot-wire a car. Maybe I'd be a car thief in the fall.

According to the clipping, the Jennings mansion was located in an exclusive area called Westerly Manor, halfway between the small towns of Georgine and Four Trees. I went through Georgine but the first road to the left led me to a farm. I hurried the bug out of there; farmers get up early and light was beginning to touch the skies in soft shades of purple. The second turnoff went to a place called Camper's Haven. Scratch that. The third was a dead end, and this trip was beginning to remind me of my phone calls, only now I was playing road roulette.

I got to Four Trees. Nothing is ever simple, but I found another road after making a few turns that led back to Georgine. Bingo! About a mile past Four Trees there was a sign saying Westerly Manor. I turned right and came to a crossroad. Oh, ho! It was called Mansion Drive. It didn't matter to me which way I turned. I figured I'd follow it up and down, back and forth, until I found the house. Even rich people have to have mailboxes.

The hot Texas sun was hurrying that morning, and it was almost daylight when my dimmed headlights picked up the fancy lettering on a quaint old box. I almost slapped on my brakes, but just in time I saw a tiny guardhouse behind the wrought-iron gates that were set into a stone wall.

I didn't know if there was a guard there or not, so I kept on driving. About two miles later, I came to the next mansion and turned the car around. The stone wall had looked formidable, but not a real problem. I stopped about eighty feet before the gate and checked it out. There was a space between two very large trees with low-hanging branches. I drove the bug in, over weeds and bunches of daylilies. I cut some tender shoots from bushes nearby with my knife to cover the bug. There was a patch of blue showing from the road, but I didn't think it mattered. I wouldn't be gone long. Little did I know.

My plan, as far as it had gotten in my mind, was to make sure that Stacy was in the house, then alarm some officials. It started going badly as soon as I climbed onto the roof of the bug to peep over the stone wall. Dogs. I guess I should have guessed.

They were yipping and yapping from a distance; they weren't right under my peeping nose. My sneaks didn't grip the bug right, either. Morning dew had made the roof slippery. It was either falling off or poking a leg over the wall. I poked. The dogs yammered more. My left foot slipped on the wet surface and I hauled it up to join my right. Crouched on the wall, I heard the dogs again and knew they were penned. There couldn't have been a guard in the guardhouse, either, for surely I'd be facing a drawn gun at that moment.

"What the heck," I muttered. "Keep going, Murphy."

The mansion was about a quarter of a mile from the road, and I kept to overgrown bushes most of the time. That was easy; the whole estate seemed overgrown. A shame, I thought, when I saw the house. It looked seedy with weeds climbing all over it. Yet there was the elegance of a castle about it. One of those romantic ones in old storybooks about princesses, and princes slaying dragons to win their hands.

It had turrets and do-hickeys, and I wondered why it had been downplayed by the press. Sleeping Beauty and Walt Disney could live there quite happily.

Silly me, I thought. I was being romantic. "Sleeping Beauty, indeed!" I swear I only mumbled but the dogs began to howl. Sickening sounds as if they couldn't wait to tear an intruder apart. Me?

I approached the house from the northwest where a long winding drive circled around a fountain then went under a portico. It was easy to imagine it filled with limousines. No one had come out of the big, wonderfully carved wood front doors, though. Even though the dogs were still howling. Lack of servants, I guessed, feeling a bit more secure.

I eased around the mansion to the back. There was a swimming pool, set down in a hollow. It looked like a large pond. Now that it was daylight and the Texas sun was stinging my skin, I would have loved to have taken a dip.

The dogs did not agree with me. They were dying to get out and kill me. I kept on going, finding myself, after a time, outside the kitchen window. There were steps and a door too, but I crept past them to look into the window. A woman, inside, had her back to me, but her voice floated outside past the screen of the open window. "I don't care how sleepy you are. If you don't feed those dogs, I will. And I'll give them chocolate cake!" She listened to the reply then sighed. "Oh, all right. But the next time you go out with the boys, I'll lock the door and throw away the key! Again." She threw the phone onto its hook and stomped on squeaky shoes to another room. She came out again, swearing, with a large bag of dog food which she opened, then squeaked across to the door.

I hugged the house. If she'd turned slightly she would have seen me, but the industrial strength of the bag took all her willpower. She tottered down the steps, yelling, "All right! I'm coming! Shut up!"

As soon as I saw her back, I was up the stairs into the kitchen. There was bacon draining on paper towels near the stove. The sharp, salty smell lingered in the air and my stomach wanted some with a rumble. "Forget it," I threatened it.

The breakfast nook was done in cool beiges and yellow. Next to it was the morning room. Not all that exciting. It had a writing desk and loungey sort of chairs. Then the formal dining room. It had immense clunky furniture, and the table was set with a single place, most likely for David Jennings. Shoot, I would've eaten a McMuffin down by the pool. I silently warned my stomach to stop grumbling, and looked for the stairs.

It was a far piece down a long hallway that entered onto another, larger area with chairs and flowers in fat vases. I guessed it was a waiting room for unwelcome guests, and I guessed the tall sliding doors on either side led to the other rooms.

One paper had mentioned an elevator being installed when Old Man Jennings had gotten sick, and when I saw the stairs, I knew why. They wound upward, centered in the waiting room and framed by banisters. I whipped up them, my sneaks sinking into a plusher carpet than at Sylvan Glade.

On the second floor, there was a vast gallery with several portraits of forbidding people who had never learned to say "Cheese!"

There were flowers, too, and a quiet museum atmosphere. I got chills when the eyes of those portraits watched me walking down the hall to the next set of stairs. I passed the elevator doors, not having the vaguest idea where on the ground floor it came out, but I wasn't taking a tour.

When I was on the third floor, I hesitated. Would her uncle hide her in her own room? No, I thought not, but opened a few doors very quietly. One, a pretty room in blues and moss greens, struck me as right. It was unoccupied. Another door showed me a rumpled bed, and I heard noises from the bathroom of splashing water and a male voice humming! David Jennings! Scared, I shut the door quietly. Pretty stupid, I thought, as I found the stairs up to the servants' quarters, hidden from view in an alcove. I'd gotten so caught up in the house, and the search, that I'd forgotten David Jennings lived there. It was a mistake I wouldn't make again, I decided, and was wrong, again.

The rooms for the servants were dormitorylike, and the bathrooms had many sinks, showers and toilet stalls. There were cobwebs, and dust covered everything. At least there weren't any ghosts of the servants around; they would have kept things clean.

I really wanted to give it up then, to get out of that house and go back to my own. It was 6:30 a.m. and Dad wouldn't get up for another hour. I needed only twenty minutes to get home, park, and climb up the tree. The two tower rooms were still left. I could check them out and still make it home in time.

They were only half a staircase up, and the first one made me smile with delight. Exquisite dolls sat on shelves, a rocking horse, moldy and old, yet still adorable, was tethered to a fat teddy bear dressed in cowboy clothes, and books were piled up on the window seats. A collection of windup toys made me want to play with them. Other stuffed toys that had been loved by children of years gone by lay with soft eyes open and unblinking.

In the sea of disaster that I'd been swimming in, the room almost cast a spell over me. I sighed. I had to go on searching, although I was sure it was stupid to. The real Stacy was in Sylvan Glade and I was being pigheaded.

The tower room had two doors besides the one I'd come through. The first led to a tiny bathroom with no towels, and the second a closet full of costumes, most brittle with age. No Stacy.

The Eye of the Storm 133

I almost didn't go to the other tower room. It was on the opposite side of the house, and I kept thinking about the young David Jennings. He might have played in that nursery, with the toys, the spectacular view and the sunny atmosphere. No child raised with that magic place could grow up and do the things I was mentally accusing him of doing.

Dragging myself down the hall of the fourth floor, I knew I'd finish the job of looking, then I'd give it up. Forever.

Nobody could possibly believe what I didn't believe myself! Stacy was in the second tower room! Bound by ropes to the bed. And it had an iron bedstead, too. I felt like I was in a clichéd movie! Her green eyes were terrified, and she couldn't speak because her mouth was bound by gauze.

I crossed the room with angry steps and pulled the gauze off. She winced with pain. "Sorry," I apologized. "I was right—I was so sure that, and now—you do have green eyes!"

"You!" The eyes that I was so happy to see widened. "From the hospital!"

Her voice was slow and muddled. She'd been drugged, for sure. "Yeah, me, from the hospital. You remember me?"

"Of course. You and Jeremiah were the only ones who knew I was out—Jeremiah isn't, can't, tell things right. While I've been lying here, after Uncle took me, I hoped, prayed you would do something! Call Todd, even if I was so..."

"Never mind." I went back to close the door and took my trusty Girl Scout knife from my jeans pocket to saw at the ropes. "We've got to get you out of here." The knife made some inroads; Stacy moved her foot to help. "Please, before I faint from curiosity, tell me what happened. How did you get away from the sanitorium? No, tell me first what happened with your uncle?"

"He—he lied." She shut her eyes for a second, then blinked them open. "I'm sorry. He drugs me all the time and I get so sleepy. Last night, I spit it out and he laughed. He said one pill didn't make much difference."

"Yep," I said, "if you've been drugged for a long time, it takes a long time to get it out of your system." I had her feet free and went to the cords tying her hands.

"He's crazy for money," she said. "That night at dinner, he was so sweet. Said he'd forgiven me and wanted me to have a really terrific wedding. I went upstairs to make out an invitation list, then I started feeling weird. He must have given me something that made me aware, but unable to move. I remember him standing over my writing desk, with a butcher's knife. I asked him what he was doing, and he said, 'Hold this for me a second.' I did; I don't know why. Then he said, 'Watch.' He was wearing plastic gloves and he plunged the knife into his stomach. The blood! He dripped it over my nightgown, then some on the bed, and left. I thought it was a nightmare, because somehow I made it to bed and that's where the police found me. The trail of blood they followed had been from my room, not to my room." Exhausted, she lay back on her pillow, one hand free now to feel her lips where the gauze had been pulled away. "Then, the day of the hurricane—you see, Dragon Lady Boden had let me have a TV, so I knew about it. She's so strange. I never knew whether she believed Uncle David or not."

"We'll talk about that later." I'd gotten through the last of the ropes. "Can you walk?"

"In a minute. As soon as the circulation returns." She swung her legs over the bed, wiggling her toes. "So anyway, she sent Jeremiah up to stay with me because he's so frightened of storms and he was in the way, upsetting the other patients who go bonkers during a storm. When he came to my room, he left the door open. I slipped out by the back staircase. I ran and ran, then the tree hit me, and there I was in the hospital where I saw you. I was just beginning to relax, to think I'd escaped, when Uncle David came into my room, dressed like a doctor and laughing. He said I'd never get away from him. I cried out, but no one heard me. He told me to shut up, and said when I died in that hospital, no one would think anything of it—he already had a replacement for me in the wings. I still don't understand that."

She tried to push herself off the bed, then stopped. I hadn't seen the door open. She gasped, and I turned. The tall man was leaning against the doorframe with a nonchalant air. I stared straight into his eyes, remembering them from the night in the hospital.

"David Jennings, I'd know you anywhere," I said with more guts than I thought I had.

"Perhaps you'd better call me *Mister* Jennings, as long as you're able."

Chapter Fourteen

A few minutes later, David Jennings threw me in the closet of the first tower room. I was bound and gagged, as Stacy had been. There was no doubt in my mind that he meant to kill both of us. All the tender thoughts I'd had of him playing in the nursery had been corrected by his kicking out at the teddy bear when he'd stormed across the nursery with me over his shoulder.

He dumped me into the closet and laughed when he told me I could have all the rats, mice and Texas roaches for breakfast that I wanted.

Swell, great, and I wanted to kill him. He'd put me on a chair with only my feet bound while I watched him tie Stacy back to the bed.

I could only guess the time that went by while I was being stifled for air in that closet. It was impossible to raise my arm to see my watch, and I couldn't have seen it anyway in the dark. Finally, by leaning against a wall and bringing my knees up to my chin, I wasn't uncomfortable. I must have dozed a bit. The lack of air and the smell of mothballs from the costumes gave me a terrible headache. When I woke up, the headache was still with me.

I kicked at the door. I needed to do something! It was solid so I shifted around to kick at the wall, hoping I could break through. The slamming of doors and loud, angry talk filtered through from outside the playroom. I stopped kicking to listen.

The voices came closer! I wanted to call attention to myself but I wanted to listen, too. I heard one voice clearly; he was right outside the closet! "I don't believe you!" he yelled. "If she was at Sylvan Glade, Dr. Boden would have let me see her. Just to shut me up. She wouldn't because she couldn't! That kid was right. Where is Stacy? Tell me, or I'll beat it out of you."

There was a scuffle, someone was knocked against the closet door. "You're crazy. As crazy as your precious Stacy. I'm calling the police now, and I'll have you arrested for assault. Now, get out of here!"

I felt more than knew that there was a heavy body pressed against the closet door. I started kicking at it, there was some more movement outside and I heard, "Call the police! Go ahead, call them. No! I'll call them myself. I don't care if they are in your pocket. Someone will listen to me. The state police. You can't have bought everyone off!"

"Todd, stop it. I can't breathe." The smothered voice of David Jennings told me he was being choked. And Todd! Todd Lewis had come to the rescue after all. I kicked harder, and prayed for him to look in the closet. Please.

Todd's voice was farther away; he must have been at the door of the playroom. "I'll be back, you scum. I'll be back with armed guards, if I have to hire them myself."

David Jennings coughed, then he yelled, "And I'll be here! With my own gun, and I'll shoot as soon as I see you!"

Oh, boy. I was still stuck. How long does it take to kill a person? Two seconds, or thereabouts, depending on the method. I stopped my futile kicking, knowing I was left alone with David Jennings again.

He opened the door. "Thought I didn't hear you? I did, and you're going to pay for it."

It had been an act he'd put on for Todd. He was breathing normally, and yet he'd gotten rid of Todd by pulling it. I was sure Todd was away from the house by now, seeking the police or whatever. Todd had bought it, and not gone to the second tower room.

I stared up at David Jennings. He reached down, grabbed me by my bound hands and dragged me upright. He had to untie the ropes from around my legs so that I could walk. Down the hall we went, and up the other steps, where he freed Stacy from her bed, then retied her hands. She looked at me helplessly, and I wished I could tell her that Todd had been there.

We got a ride in the elevator. Jennings couldn't get the two of us downstairs any other way. Big deal.

The doors opened out into a hallway I hadn't seen, but it must have been near enough the kitchen for David Jennings to yell, "Anita, Ralph! Come here, I need some help!"

Besides everything else, the man was lazy, too. Stacy and I were lightweights compared to him.

The Eye of the Storm

The woman I'd seen before came running. "Ralph is out feeding the dogs," she said nervously, seeing the two of us bound up like that.

I wished I could've told Jennings she was lying. The tape on my mouth was beginning to hurt, too, and I felt like there were pure wool socks in my mouth.

Anita, the woman, helped Jennings take us into the kitchen. When we were propped up on chairs, he said, "I'm going to find Ralph, and if he's still in bed, sleeping off a hangover, both of you are out on your ears." All of us were happy to see him slam out of the kitchen door. I knew that because Anita was looking at the floor, studying its crisscrossed pattern. The tension didn't leave the room, but it eased a bit. Then Anita went to Stacy. "I'm gonna be in big trouble for this, but I can't stand to see you..." She ripped off the tape on Stacy's mouth.

"Ouch," Stacy muttered. Whew, I felt for her. The second time in a very short while she'd had that done to her. "Oh, thanks. Thank you, Anita. Can you help? I need to go to the bathroom. Awful. Now."

"Oh, honey, I can't do that." Anita pushed her mousy brown hair out of her eyes. "Your uncle...?"

"Please, I'm going to be sick," Stacy pleaded.

Anita dithered and fussed, asking Stacy if she was sure. Stacy bent over with what appeared to be very painful cramps. "All right, all right." Anita reached for the kitchen shears, hanging on a nail by the door. She freed Stacy with quick snips, and Stacy rose, stumbled and almost fell. Anita propped her up, and Stacy reached for the jar from the table we'd been sitting by. *Smash!* Anita lay unconscious on the floor, among large pieces of broken pottery and chocolate chip cookies.

There is no word for what I felt. I'd believed in Stacy. When I saw her give Anita such a blow, I thought maybe she'd done the same to her uncle with a knife.

Then *she* got the scissors and came for me. "Don't be silly," she said, seeing that I was frightened. "The only homicidal maniac we have to fear is my blasted uncle. And if he gets back here before we're gone, we're dead in the water, get my drift?"

She pulled the tape off my mouth, and with smarting lips I sucked in air. Then she cut my ropes. "Move it. We've got to hit the road—no, wait!" I was already at the kitchen door. I waited, watching her warily. There was a pile of clean laundry on top of a dryer in the far corner of the kitchen. She scattered it, looking at the garments and choosing a man's T-shirt and some faded jeans. Then she grabbed a string bag from a drawer and leaned over to throw some cookies into it.

"What are you doing, packing lunch?" I asked, sure that Jennings would be back any second.

She didn't answer me until we were outdoors and halfway across the lawn. "The cookies are for the dogs," she explained hurriedly as we ran, "and if you think I want to be rescued in my nightgown, you're mistaken."

"Quick thinking," I admitted. I'd forgotten that she was wearing a skimpy cotton shift. "Do we really have to stop by the kennels?" No, I didn't want to.

"I raised Sweets and Whoopie! If I give them cookies and tell them not to kill us, they might listen. Uncle has had them for five years, though, and he might have switched commands on me. Just like he switched everything else in my life around."

We'd skirted around the swimming pool by then and were at the fence of the kennels. Stacy shoved her bundle of clothes at me and took several cookies out of the string bag, holding some through the holes in the wire. "Hi, Sweets, hi, Whoops, it's only me. You remember me, don't you?"

They stopped yimmering and yapping and came cautiously forward. She made gestures with her left hand and crumbled cookies with her right. I don't care if she did raise them, they were ugly. I've never cared too much for Dobermans. When they got to the fence, they ate the cookies and licked her hand. "Good boys, good. You're both so good. Now, lie down. Roll over. Play dead." They did. "Okay." She looked at me. "That's all I can do now. We'd better get going. Bye, Sweets, bye, Whoops, don't follow us, okay?" They woofed in reply and she threw in some more cookies, but not all of them. "C'mon." She tugged at my arm. "Let's get out of here."

Too soon those dogs were yapping again. From a distance, though, because Stacy and I were deep in the woods. We'd stopped for a breather, and I'd had a chance to ask her where we were going. "If we can get another mile through the woods, there's a place in the stone wall that I used to go over. It comes out right near Georgine. There's this guy I used to meet." She averted her eyes from me, and seemed embarrassed. "Anyway, he'll help us."

"You must have wanted to see him pretty bad," I said.

"No, not really. It was another excuse to get away from Uncle David, but Ron will help us, I'm sure, I think."

How I wanted to ask which it was, sure or think. I kept my mouth shut, though. Stacy was my guide through the thick growth between trees that loomed above us, cutting off most of the sun. Stacy reached out a hand for mine. "It looks worse than it is. I used to do this at night. I had a flashlight, though. Anyway, there's a creek about forty feet down there and, if you don't mind, we'll dunk ourselves in water, then I'll change clothes. That should throw the dogs off the scent."

I had my sneaks on, but Stacy was barefoot, and before we got to the creek she had a run-in with a jagged branch. By the time we got to the little brook, the cut was bleeding. She put on the jeans and T-shirt, both of which hung loosely on her, and I made her sit down so I could wrap her foot with my socks. My knife had been taken by her uncle, of course, but I tore up the nightshirt and bound both feet with it. "That'll help a little," I said.

"Thanks," she croaked. "No one's been kind to me for a long, long time. Why are you?"

I saw some tears glittering in the green eyes, and her tone was wistful. "I'll explain it all later," I said, hearing the dogs getting nearer. "I have to tell you—Todd was in the house today. It was only by chance he didn't get to your, er, uh, room."

"He was?" Stacy gathered her strength. "I thought he'd forgotten all about me."

"Nope." I hated hearing the sounds of those dogs. Stacy seemed like, well, an okay sort of person. "Those dogs...?"

"Right." She threw some cookies on the far bank of the creek. Then she ate one, and passed one to me. "Hope it gives us some energy. I feel so sleepy."

"Eat some more," I said, wishing I didn't have to. My stomach had a parade of bongo drums in it. Stacy, though, had been drugged for a time, and I thought I remembered reading somewhere that sugar helped. I made a note to check it out, if we got out of this.

"We have to keep on," she said sleepily. "After the creek, it's only another quarter of a mile. I'm sorry."

"For what?"

"For getting you involved in this whole thing."

"You want me to slap you up side the head? Let's just get out of here."

"Maybe if you slapped me, I'd wake up."

"Is that a joke? I thought rich people didn't have a sense of humor."

"Who said. If I didn't have one, I would have gone to la-la land a long time ago."

"Okey-doke." I supported her for only a few paces, then she seemed to wake up and take charge.

The dogs had been put off the scent. I heard them whining in confusion behind us, and the sounds of sharp commands from rough voices penetrated through the woods in a frightening way. We weren't far enough away from the creek, yet, not to hear them.

The lush growth felt like a trap, and when we came to a clearing, I breathed a sigh of relief. "Ssst." Stacy took my arm and whispered, "See that fallen tree? Right past there, we go back into the woods and make a turn to the left. Only a few feet, and we're there."

We were almost to the tree, blinking in the sudden sunlight and running over daisies and wildflowers, when the dogs came rough and tumbling into the clearing. "No!" I looked back at them.

"Don't say anything. Let's get to the wall, then let me deal with them."

With pleasure, I thought, gritting my teeth and turning left. One of the dogs skirted past Stacy and came snarling at me just as I got to the stone wall. "Stacy!" I hollered, as the dog sank his fangs into my ankle.

"Don't move," she said quietly, holding the other dog by his collar. He was still licking crumbs off his face, and was nuzzling Stacy for more cookies. "Sweets," Stacy said with authority. "Heel. Now."

She let go of Whoopie's collar to reach into the bag and pull out the last few cookies. "Here you go, both of you." She threw the cookies as far away from us as she could, and Sweets let go of my ankle. I was paralyzed. "C'mon." Stacy shook my arm. "We're almost out of here."

I glanced down at my ankle and saw fang marks in my jeans. The dog had gotten mostly fabric, not flesh. That was a relief, but the stone wall wasn't. "How'd you get up that thing?"

"My, er, friend, er, came in and made stepping-stones. See?" I nodded. They were covered with moss, and just visible. "He carved a hole above each rock, oh never mind." She heard the voices at the same time I did. Both masculine, one definitely Jennings, and both calling for the dogs. "Come on, you first. I'll be right behind you if you fall."

I wanted to ask if she ever had, but there was no time. I started climbing. The footholds were easy enough to find, but they were slippery, and when I heard the dogs yelping back near us, I almost slipped. Stacy took my foot and shoved it back. "Ouch!" She'd squeezed my bitten ankle.

She was following me spiderlike, so closely that the next time I slipped she could push me by my fanny back on course. I was up, though, on a wide stone ledge, and soon she was beside me. The climb up had been about fifteen feet, but the stone wall was set into a five-foot

The Eye of the Storm

ditch, making the climb down twenty. The dogs were below us, whining again, probably looking for more cookies.

"He did the same on this side. I'll go first. Just watch." She made it all look easy; I fell on my rear end about three-quarters of the way down. "You okay?" She picked me up.

"Some rescuer I make," I said ruefully, brushing myself off.

We were standing in the ditch, and she hugged me. "Honey, you're the best rescuer I've ever had."

"The only one, dont'cha mean?"

"I don't even know your name."

Since I'd first seen her tied to the bed, I hadn't taken a good look at her, except for the eyes, of course. They were her whole face practically, since the rest of her features were even and regular.

I looked up at the gauze of the bandage on her head. The short, beige hair sprouted around it. "Tessa," I said. "How do you feel? Any headaches or anything?"

"Oh, you mean the operation?" Her hand flew to the gauze. "I must look a sight, but I feel wonderful being outside. Tessa. That's a nice..." She stopped, hearing the dogs again, and the voices.

"They must have gone over the wall," Jennings was yelling.

The other, the one who answered, had a raspy voice. "I'll go after them, Mis-ter Jennings, sir. You take the dogs back to the house and git over to Georgine by car."

"Don't give me orders, you stupid drunk. I'm going over—I've got the gun. You meet me in Georgine."

Stacy's mouth opened, her eyes filled with terror. This time I took her hand, hauled her out of the ditch.

We crossed the road and landed in the ditch on the other side, hiding in grass dotted with wildflowers. "Stacy, are you all right?"

Now it was she who was paralyzed. "It's okay. You got me out of there, I'll get you out of here. I've got to know where the nearest phone is."

"The police..." She gulped. "They won't listen. Uncle David has them all paid off."

"That's what Todd said. He was going to call the state police, and that's what I'm going to do, right after I call my father. It'll be better to have him know where we are, in case the state police screw up. Now, which way to Georgine?"

"We'd better stick to the ditch. Nobody can see us from the road, but it'll get kind of unpleasant."

Unpleasant was an understatement. The ditch ran right into a sewage run that had wet, mucky muck. Around us, above the ditch, was clover, corn and daisies, but we were knee-deep in mud.

A quarter of a mile later, we climbed out of the ditch and hid in the cornfield, watching the road for any signs of David Jennings.

We were hunkered down, and the flies attacked us. I'm sure there were other bugs too, but I didn't want to think about them. What with Stacy's foot and my ankle, we were not too fit. We did have a clear view of the road, though. And we saw David Jennings walking along it, looking here and there.

"He's slow," Stacy said. "By the time he gets to Georgine, we can make the calls and git. If we run. Can you?"

"Yeah." And we ran. Through the cornfield to where it ended and the town began. Stacy led me past the back ends of small and large houses, through gardens and yards. A tiny pond had dragonflies, nits, yet goldfish flickered their orange fins as we ran past it.

"Ron works in the gas station." Stacy stopped by the edge of what seemed to be a junkyard. It was only a storing place for the back of Tiggle's Garage. "You liked a guy called Ron Tiggle?"

Stacy made a giggling sound. "I thought middle-class people didn't have a sense of humor."

"I would have gone to la-la... whoops." David Jennings was there. Past the junkyard and in the paved area behind the garage.

There was a stocky man with him, and there were the dogs. The stocky man weaved back and forth, as though drunk. "That's Ralph," Stacy whispered. "He's had a belt or two, or three, but he made record time picking up Uncle David."

"Now what?" We were hiding behind the remains of an old Buick.

"We wait. They're waiting, probably for Ron or his father. The dogs are leashed, see, and they can't possibly smell us when there are all the good gassy smells around."

I wished I felt that confident, yet I had to admit Stacy was right. They wanted to go everywhere, except toward us.

Pretty soon, a middle-aged guy with tattoos on his muscular arms joined Ralph and Jennings. He apologized. "I didn't know you was coming, Mister Jennings. I had to go tow Bantnor's tractor outta the field. She would try to run that farm. What can I do for you?"

He was wearing a shirt that showed all the tattoos, along with his muscles. It was tattered, as if on purpose. "If you'd stop fooling around with the women, like your son, we'd do better business," David Jennings said.

"Yessir," Tiggle said. "I still hafta thank you for that. Not for you, Ron'd still be here, but now he's a real bonafie cippa."

I looked at Stacy and there were tears welling in her eyes again. "I wondered why he didn't come forward, to tell that I didn't care about the money. Now he's a certified public accountant, caring about all sorts of money."

"Shhh." She'd talked too loudly. The dogs were curious. They hear better than most humans. "Keep it down, okay?"

The dogs had picked us up. They were straining their leashes toward us. Ralph drew them back when Tiggle said, "That's only them rabbits diggin' in me garden out back."

We'd missed some of the conversation when Stacy had her crying spell, because Tiggle seemed to know what Jennings was talking about when he said, "Right, sir, if I see them, I'll holler." He walked them through the garage.

"We could hit him with something." I eyed the tire iron next to the garage.

"No," Stacy said. "The rabbit thing was a signal. He doesn't have a garden, and he always liked me."

Waiting again, I felt like mosquito fodder. They and the blue-bottomed flies bombed us. Eventually, Tiggle came back out into the yard. He tinkered with this and that, then yelled, "Alle-In-Free! Stacy, 'chile, you out there?"

Stacy had tears in her eyes as she hugged Tiggle. I had tears in my eyes as I phoned my house and got Mom. It turned out that my father and Max had been looking for me since almost daybreak. It also turned out that Stacy's Ron had been the only one to take money from Jennings. Tiggle, his father, had never approved, and had always thought Stacy innocent.

Chapter Fifteen

The state cops took our statement, and screamed out of Tiggle's to find David Jennings and Ralph. Dad and Max had brought Todd Lewis with them, and both he and Stacy were touching, laughing, and crying at the same time. Dad insisted we go to the hospital, where Stacy was admitted and my dog bite was treated. It was pretty superficial, but both Sweets and Whoopie would be tested for rabies.

I held Stacy's hand as Gail Robbins wheeled the wheelchair. By then Jennings, Ralph and Anita had been arrested. "Are you sure?" Stacy asked.

"When have I lied to you?" I asked.

"Never." She smiled. Her foot had been bound up and the bandage on her head redone, yet she was so happy. "You're the only person I've known who hasn't lied to me, except Todd and Tiggle."

"There're going to be a lot more," I said, as Todd joined us, to take her other hand.

Like a zombie, I went home with Dad. Mom hugged me a lot, and Dad kept saying, "I should have listened to you."

I was too tired to agree. I'd had a tetanus shot, and the awful experience had caught up to me. "Wasn't Max around there somewhere?" I asked around a big fat yawn.

"He was. As soon as he saw you were okay, he went back to the diner, but he'll be here later," Dad said, helping me upstairs.

"I have so many questions...." Another, bigger, fatter yawn came.

"Later," he said.

"No." I rubbed my eyes, sitting on the bed. "I want a bath, and some food, and then I'll be fine." I really felt like that, except I made the mistake of leaning back on my pillows. That was the last thing I remember before I passed out.

It was still light when I woke up, and at first I thought I'd only slept a few hours. That, however, did not make sense. My clock radio said that it was four o'clock, and it had been 4:30 when I'd gotten home from the hospital. I scrunched up my eyes, shook my head and looked at the clock again. Oh, no! What if it'd all been a dream?

Sitting up, I looked at my leg and saw the small bandage. I wasn't wearing jeans anymore, though. I was in my regular nightshirt. And I didn't feel grubby. I was clean and starving. I could have eaten anything, even Tizzy who slept with me.

"You're awake!" Mom bustled in with a tray of tea sandwiches, crusts cut off and elegant looking. There was a huge pitcher of iced tea, too. "How do you feel?" She put the tray on my window table.

"Sore," I said, now feeling bruises, bumps and aching muscles. "Did—er—did all that happen?"

"You bet your sweet fanny it did, and if it ever happens again, I'll whup the skin offa it."

"Don't pick on me. I hurt enough."

"I mean it, though. Don't you ever do anything like that again."

"How long did I sleep?" I asked, to change the subject before she made me promise. After all, who knew?

"Almost twenty-four hours," she said. "You'd better get up and eat those sandwiches. Max made them especially for you."

"Max?" I grinned. "Where is he?"

"Downstairs, cooking his little heart out. We're having Beef Wellington for dinner. He threw me out of my own kitchen! He's dicing, blanching and whatever down there."

"Beef Wellington? Is the boy normal?"

"He's so normal it's disgusting."

She sat with me while I devoured the tiny sandwiches and drank the whole pitcher of iced tea. "I wonder how Stacy is."

"Waiting for your call, I'm afraid." Mom jumped up and brought the phone to the table. "I've talked to her about three times today already. She seems like a nice girl—I'm glad you rescued her. You know the number of the hospital. I'll be downstairs, sitting at the feet of the boy chef. Seems I've been going to the wrong farmers' market, too."

My phone was back! Hurrah. Yet, I was slow to punch the number. It's funny calling someone you might never have known except for the small detail of

The Eye of the Storm 153

saving her life and then having her save yours in return. I wouldn't have known how to begin if she hadn't answered saying, "This better be you, Tessa Murphy, or I'm going to hang up."

"It's me." I giggled. We talked for about fifteen minutes, and she cleared up some of the details I hadn't known. The night she escaped from Sylvan Glade, nondoctor Boden had called Jennings as soon as she knew. Jennings and Ralph were scouting the area in separate cars. Ralph had spotted her being taken into the ambulance after the tree fell on her. Jennings had, of course, hit her in the hospital, with the lamp. Any patient's condition is given out on the phone, but they didn't know what name she was using, so Ralph hung around the hospital, watching and waiting for a corpse to be removed. No such luck. He'd admitted to stealing her from the recovery room.

Then I got into the act. David Jennings had seen my name tag that night, and when Dr. Waite called Boden for the appointment, she checked with Jennings. They set up the phony Stacy together.

"Who was she—is she?" I asked.

"As near as I can gather, she's a former patient whose funds had been cut off, and she was in the state mental hospital. My affairs are going to be a mess for a while, because until Uncle—until David Jennings is prosecuted, and convicted, he has control."

"Still? That's so unfair!"

"It's okay. The police say that Ralph has confessed, and it's only a matter of time before my ex-uncle does, too. The point I was trying to make is that I'll help out with the phony Stacy. I know what it's like."

"Yeah. What about Jeremiah?"

"They let him come to see me! He was my only friend, you know? And I'm not going to let anything happen to him. I'll keep him in chocolates for the rest of his life!"

Then Stacy went on to tell me that it had been Ralph who'd tried to run me down that day, and who'd been outside the house that night. But Dr. Boden had set up the phone calls to Dad the following day. She was also under arrest for conspiracy to commit a felony. "I'm ashamed of Todd for treating you like that."

"Oh, Stace, he made up for it, didn't he?" I said. "By the way, how did that happen?"

It was simple. Since he knew my name, and Boden had told him Dad's, he'd called the hospital for Dr. John Murphy's address. When he arrived, demanding to talk to me, Max, Dad and Mom were already pacing the floor, wondering where I'd gone. Stacy didn't know much more than that, except that somehow, they went back to the mansion.

We talked for a few minutes more, and she told me some news that I loved. When we hung up, I had the feeling that Stacy and I were going to be friends for a long time, maybe forever.

After a long bath, I dressed in some of my new clothes and went downstairs to stuff myself. Then Max and I pulled two chaises together outside and cuddled. He filled in the rest. "When Todd showed up here, we were all fit to be tied. He said he'd been out to the mansion and thought Stacy was hidden there, but he hadn't found her. I remembered the clippings and thought you'd think that was a real good idea, too."

"Reading my mind?" I murmured. His arm was around me, and my muscles were beginning to relax.

The Eye of the Storm 155

He kissed my forehead. "If I don't, who will? Anyway, oh, I forgot, the reason I was here in the first place was because your dad called me in hysterics."

"Good, go ahead." I pictured Dad screaming at Max on the phone.

"Okay, to make a long story short, we drove past the mansion about four times before I saw that flash of blue through the trees. Next time, don't hide that ugly bug so well." He kissed me again. "Todd had an old key to the gates. We got in, and found that Anita staggering around, swearing about you, Stacy, Ralph and Jennings. So we found out what had happened, but not where you were. By then, you'd called your mother from the gas station, and we called her right after, and that's it. I think it's so neat that Stacy wants you to be maid of honor at her wedding to Todd, though."

"Me too." I'd announced that bit of news between great gulps of Beef Wellington at dinner. "I feel like I've rescued a real-life princess who's going to marry her prince and live happily ever after." I paused, then added, "Of course I'll probably get grounded. But I'm going to that wedding if I have to go down the tree again!"

* * * * *

I must have been asleep for about an hour when I heard it on the door, a soft knock as though the person didn't want to wake up anyone but me.

"Who is it?" I called out in a loud whisper.

I sat as still as I could trying to decide what to do. It wasn't hot in the room, but I could feel a cold sweat on the back of my neck.

What was on the other side of the door? I didn't think it was something I wanted to meet.

Monica's going to find out who or what is lurking behind that closed door. She's in for a real shock!

Read all about it in

SHOCK EFFECT
by
Glen Ebisch

Coming from Crosswinds in November.

Did you hear about the war on flab?

My flab! Well, my mom, who's a gorgeous movie star, decided she couldn't have a fatso for a daughter. So she tried all kinds of stuff. Do I need to tell you that NOTHING WORKED? I didn't get skinny, I just got mad. And when I get mad, watch out....

Bigger is Better

SHEILA SCHWARTZ

Coming from Crosswinds in October

COMING NEXT MONTH FROM CROSSWINDS™

SHOCK EFFECT
By Glen Ebisch

Being a waitress in a summer hotel can be more than just hard work, as Monica found out when she discovered a corpse in a bedroom. Was it murder?

KALEIDOSCOPE
By Candice Ransom

Cress and Darien find that life is a mysterious design of changing patterns. After initial misunderstandings, they decide to explore it together.

AVAILABLE THIS MONTH

THE EYE OF THE STORM
Susan Dodson

BIGGER IS BETTER
Sheila Schwartz

Wow!

A whole book about Sylvia Smith-Smith! Hot off the pages of *Seventeen* magazine. As usual, Sylvia is shrewd, cool and a little weird.

> "Urgent! Urgent! Wake up the President. The earth is about to collide with the sun!"
>
> "Gentlemen, gentlemen, let him sleep—he couldn't handle this anyway. This looks like a job for... Sylvia Smith-Smith!"
>
> "But, General, she's only a teenager."
>
> "Yes, but she's got a good head on her shoulders."

SYLVIA SMITH-SMITH by Peter Nelson. Available from Crosswinds in September.

Grab it before your friends beat you to it.

SYLVIA-1

ATTRACTIVE, SPACE SAVING BOOK RACK

Display your most prized novels on this handsome and sturdy book rack. The hand-rubbed walnut finish will blend into your library decor with quiet elegance, providing a practical organizer for your favorite hard-or soft-covered books.

Only $9.95

Approximately 16" x 8" when assembled

Assembles in seconds!

To order, rush your name, address and zip code, along with a check or money order for $10.70* ($9.95 plus 75¢ postage and handling) payable to *Crosswinds*.

Crosswinds
Book Rack Offer
901 Fuhrmann Blvd.
P.O. Box 1396
Buffalo, NY 14269-1396

Offer not available in Canada.

*New York and Iowa residents add appropriate sales tax.